# Away to Me

*For Randy —*

## Kathy Wagenknecht

*Kathy Wagenknecht*

*Away to Me* is a work of fiction. Names, places, and incidents are products of the author's imagination or are used fictitiously

Copyright © 2011 by Kathy Wagenknecht
All rights reserved
Published by White Wagon Books

CreateSpace Edition

Cover painting: Pat White

ISBN-13: 978-1-46-104700-1
ISBN-10: 1-46-104700-5

Printed in the United States of America

**For Pat, without whom….**

*Special thanks to*

*The Blackbird Academy Gang for encouragement and good humor*

*and*

*my proofreaders and cheerleaders: Karen, Linda, Rita, Suzann, Merry and Pam*

# Prologue

*April 4, 1960*
*Dodge City, Kansas*

Where the hell is Matt Dillon when you need him?

I came to this place looking for safety. I guess I thought Matt and Chester would be walking around on the dusty streets of Dodge City just like they do every Saturday night on "Gunsmoke."

What a fool I am.

I finally get up the nerve to run, and this is where I've come. To this windy little nothing of a town in the middle of nowhere. Here where I have no money, no job, no friends, no family, no future.

I am going to write down on this cheap stationery from the Long Branch Motel what I've done with my life so far. Maybe some day I'll be able to explain it to someone who might want to know me. If she ever finds me.

How do I describe growing up with a sweet but weak mother and an abusive-when-drunk father? Does it matter? I got through it – hiding, sneaking and lying, mostly to myself.

Somehow I turned out pretty at fifteen. Or pretty enough to attract the attention of the best-looking bad boy in the neighborhood. Johnny Benton. I thought he was my salvation.

Old story: he charmed; I gave in; I got pregnant; he disappeared.

I should have put her up for adoption. But I was afraid she'd end up with people like those who'd adopted me. So I kept her. Loved her. Tried to protect her.

Johnny drifted in and out of our lives. Sometimes leaving money. Sometimes swinging fists.

I found jobs here and there – enough money to live in a crappy rent house in a crappy part of town. Enough to feed us.

When she started to talk, Johnny scared me. He'd stare at her, clenching and un-clenching his jaws. If he hit me, I'd heal. If he hit her, he could kill her. I quit going to work when he was around. I had to keep watch. I lost my job, got behind on my rent, got an eviction notice.

Johnny disappeared.

Then a detective showed up, looking for me, carrying a letter from a woman claiming to be a relative of my real mother. She'd enclosed a money order for $100. I paid my back rent, talked my last boss into rehiring me, and settled back into my life.

Within a couple of weeks, Johnny was back. Angry. Drunk. Mean. He broke my arm, blacked my eye, and kicked me in the ribs when I threw myself over the baby. I called the detective who'd brought the letter. I told him to come – I had something to send my family.

I dressed her as good as I could, wrote the note, and hid in the yard, peeking in the window when he came. I see him carrying her away every night in the same dream I've had for three years.

Except for the nights I was too drunk to dream. Or too hurt.

Johnny tried to kill me when he found his daughter gone. I left for Chicago as soon as I got out of the hospital. My best friend in grade school had moved to Chicago. I thought…. Oh, it doesn't matter what I thought.

Now three years, five names, seven jobs and four states later, I am in the Long Branch in Dodge City.

Maybe Miss Kitty needs a new girl.


*Edie Bell*

# Part I:  The Outrun

*The outrun is the initial run of the dog, a large
semi-circular or pear-shaped path that
encompasses all the sheep to be moved.*

# Chapter 1

Absently tapping the brim of his baseball cap on the counter as he looked at the newspaper, Rusty squinted a moment, shook his head and gave a sigh. He leaned back in his chair, closed his eyes and let a slight smile play over his freckled face. He straightened up and mumbled, "I gotta get more money if I'm gonna ask Shawna to the dance." He rubbed his hand through the carrot-colored buzz cut, leaned back over the counter to look at the newspaper again, and stiffened, holding his breath.

"Hot Damn!" he exploded. Then read aloud, "BONUS! $200.00 HIRING BONUS! We're looking for smiling, happy faces for day, lunch, and evening shifts. Both weekdays and weekends, part-time and full-time. We offer free meals, free uniforms, paid training but NO GREASE! Apply in person at SUBWAY." He looked up flushed and smiling, "$200.00, Betty. I could even rent a tux. I bet she'd notice me in a tux!"

Betty, behind the counter, grinned at him, "Rusty, she'd have to be a fool not to notice you, handsome boy like you." She wiped up the ring of water that had gathered around the nearly empty Coke glass in front of Rusty. "And with your experience at Sonic, you'd be a shoo-in at Subway. Go on down there and apply!"

Rusty jumped up and ran toward the door, turned, came back to the counter and flipped down a dollar and some change, then ran back to the front of the café, nearly colliding with a small girl in tap shoes and a ruffled skirt. She dodged under his arm as he ran out the door yelling over his shoulder, "Sorry, Bitsy!"

"Bye, Uncle Rusty!" Bitsy called, tapping heels and toes in complicated, un-named rhythms on the tile floor. At five, Bitsy was all arms and legs, with elbows jutting out like sugar-bowl handles and skinned knees pumping as she put her all into her entrance dance.

"Mamma, look at this new dance I learned!"

Betty smiled at her blonde bouncy daughter, noticing her black patent tap shoes untied, her skirt drooping in back, the streak of dirt across her nose. "Honey, that's great. What did Mrs. Morris say about your routine?"

Bitsy straightened, stood still, thrust out her chest and said sternly, "Bitsy, you're trying to go too fast. Stick to the steps we've worked on." Then slumping and looking up at Betty, she whined, "But Mamma, we're just doing *baby* stuff!" She shuffled her feet, tapped a toe in front of the other, shuffled, reversed the toe tap and stopped. "See?"

Betty stifled a giggle as she looked down at the already clean counter, swiping it again with her cloth. "Bits, you've got to learn to walk before you can run. Mrs. Morris is just trying to teach you the basics. Remember how you had to learn your letters before you could write your name?"

A staccato whirlwind swept down to the end of the counter. "Oh, Mamma! You just don't unnerstand!" She whirled again and crashed into a jeans-clad butt seated on a stool, one cowboy-booted foot curled behind the supporting chrome leg.

"Oh, sorry mister!" Bitsy walked quietly back toward her mother and sat at the place Rusty had vacated. "Can I have some milk? Dancing makes me thirsty." She kicked her feet against the counter as she waited, nodding in time with the tapping noises she was making.

"So, little lady, you wanna be a tap dancer, huh?" said the wearer of the cowboy boots and jeans. His gravelly voice held a trace of Texas, that flattened twang that seemed to come natural to guys in boots, jeans, Go Rodeo t-shirts and Stetson hats.

Bitsy turned toward him to stare – this was a cowboy pure and simple. He just needed a bandana to look exactly like Toy Story's Woody. "Are you a cowboy, mister?" she asked squinting to avoid the glare coming from a plate glass window behind him.

He turned toward her, bringing his face into the light, and she saw the scar on his cheek. A crescent moon stood out white against his tan, running from under his left eye, around his cheekbone, and into the four-day stubble on his cheek.

 "Whadja do to your face? You gotta moon on it," Bitsy said as she squeezing closed her brown eye and peered at him only with her blue one.

"Bitsy!" Betty gasped then turned to the man and said, "I'm sorry. She's so curious, and her inner censor doesn't work yet."

"It's okay, ma'am. Reminds me of my sister at that age." He turned toward Bitsy, leaned an elbow on the counter and put his fingers to his scar. "Yep, guess it does look like a crescent moon. It's from a bull's hoof. Got kicked in the face once when I was bull ridin'. Lucky I didn't lose my eye."

Bitsy stared. "Why would you want to ride a bull?"

"Why do you want to tap dance?"

"Because it makes me feel like I'm flying and playing drums, and, and, happy!"

"Uh huh," he grinned, leaning back in his chair and taking a sip of coffee.

"Does riding on bulls make you happy?" Bitsy twirled her hair around a finger and played with the puddle of spilled milk.

"Used to," he said, as he got off the stool. He fished for change to lay beside his plate then carried his check and a five dollar bill to the cash register at the other end of the counter. He handed his money to Betty and said casually, "Don't know of anyone looking for help around here, do you?"

She reached under the counter and pulled out the newspaper her little brother had been reading. It was opened to the want ads, so she quickly scanned the page, looked up at him, and read aloud, "Farm Help Needed: Part-time, possibly full-time. Must have experience with poultry and cattle. Apply in person at Floyd Sales and Construction."

He fiddled with his hat, then asked, "Do ya know where Floyd Sales and Construction is?"

Betty nodded. "I guess I do. It belongs to my ex-father-in-law."

From the back corner booth, Mary Nell Floyd watched the scene playing out before her. She waggled her fingers at her granddaughter who made faces at her in the mirror. Then she sniffed the air as the cowboy walked by, noticing tobacco, sweat, dust and dog.

After the cowboy left, Mary Nell spoke to Betty, "So you sent that cowboy out to our place? Think Walter'll like him?"

Betty shrugged. "It's pretty clear that Dub won't be back, and you all need the help. It won't hurt for Walter to talk to him."

Mary Nell nodded. "At least he smells like someone used to work. Maybe he'll be okay. I hope so. There's a lot of work to do on that farm."

Bitsy squeezed her brown eye shut and squinted at Mary Nell. "Grandmary, can I come to the farm with you? I'm tired of this place."

After receiving a nod from Betty, Mary Nell walked up to Bitsy, put her hand on Bitsy's shoulder, and said, "Come on, kid. Let's blow this joint."

Bitsy looked up quizzically, then puckered up and blew.

# Chapter 2

*"I hear there's a new cowboy in town."*

*"Yeah, workin' for Floyd's."*

*"I saw him walkin' down the street. Looks fine in jeans."*

A week later, Walter Floyd yelled from his pickup toward the small house in front of him, "Buck! Buck, you in there?" A black and white blur raced from around the back of the house and hit the door of the truck with a thud. Lulu, Buck's border collie, whined at the window until Walter reached out to pet her.

Following Lulu at a much slower pace, Buck walked toward the truck and whistled Lulu back to his side. "What can I do for you, Mr. Floyd?"

"Walter. Call me Walter."

"OK, Walter. What's up?"

"First off, Mary Nell wants me to invite you up for dinner. Tonight. 6:30. OK?"

Buck looked up, startled, "Dinner? But Mr., er, Walter, you don't need to do that. I'm okay here. Even made it to the grocery store already."

"I know I don't have to, but we want to. So it's settled?"

Buck nodded, "I'll be there."

"Also want to thank you for the way you just took over with the chickens. Fixing that coop and the nesting boxes." Walter flushed, unaccustomed to giving praise.

Buck blushed in turn and shuffled a foot in the dust, "While you're here, let me ask you about the bull in the northwest pasture. Is he okay?"

"What do you mean okay? He's healthy as far as I know. Why?"

"He just seems a little too settled, I guess that's the word. He's got no curiosity about me or Lulu."

Walter closed his brown eye and squinted through the blue one at Buck. "What do you know about bulls?"

"Well, sir, I rode on 'em for about 20 years. Or tried to."

"Hmm. Well, I'll see you at 6:30," and he gunned his pickup out the dirt driveway and turned toward the big house on the hill.

"Whatcha think, Lulu girl? Think we're gonna like it here?" Buck stroked Lulu under the chin, earning an answering lick on the hand.

At 6:30 on the nose, Buck knocked on the screen door of the big yellow frame house. As he waited, he looked around and saw the table set on the porch, ready for dinner. A big pitcher of iced tea growing dewy sat at the end of the table. Just looking at that cold pitcher made him thirsty.

He'd taken some care as he cleaned up for dinner, even shaving his sandy-colored stubble and putting on his cleanest pair of jeans. He wiped his damp palms down his thighs. He didn't like to meet new people, and he thought he'd better impress Mary Nell Floyd, or he and Lulu would be asked to leave their comfortable little house.

A tall buxom woman in khaki shorts, Birkenstock sandals, and a Rainbow Coalition t-shirt opened the door. Her short gray hair and lack of makeup made her look older than her husband, but her strong handshake as she welcomed him made him rethink this first impression.

"Thanks for inviting me to dinner, ma'am." Buck removed his hand from hers and rubbed it down his thigh again.

Mary Nell shrugged and pointed at the rockers. "Have a rock and rest a bit. I'll have dinner out here in just a few minutes." As she rubbed her nose with the hand that had shaken his she noticed a slightly sweet odor. Was he wiping it on or off his thigh, she wondered.

Buck sat, rocked, rubbed his palms on his thighs, looked at the iced tea pitcher, swallowed, and finally noticed the bob-tailed black cat staring at him from the porch swing through bright green eyes.

He stood and walked over to the cat. "Hey, kitty, what happened to your tail?" he said quietly. He reached out to touch the cat's head when a voice said, "Got it caught in a tractor belt." He jerked his hand back, then he looked around sheepishly.

Mary Nell stood at the door with a big platter of fried chicken in both hands. "You sure are skittish, son. Did you think Roberta answered you?" She chuckled as she set the platter on the table and headed back inside.

"Um, no, ma'am," he mumbled after her, wondering what else he could do to make himself look foolish. He sat back down in the rocker, wiped his hands on his thighs again and leaned his head back against the chair. He let out a deep sigh then muttered under his breath, "Roberta, bob-tail. Got it."

~~~

"Whole wheat, turkey, American, with lettuce and pickles. Just mustard. Cut in half." Rusty glanced up from the condiments, hand filled with shredded lettuce, and dropped it into the pickle tub as he looked into the eyes of Shawna Taylor. Heat traveled from his chest to the top of his head, staining his skin bright red as it went. He couldn't speak. He nodded, looked down, and fished lettuce out of the pickles.

"Uh, OK," he managed. "Oh, God, Oh, God, Oh, God," he chanted quietly. He took deep breaths, trying to calm his pounding chest. "Um, Shawna. Are you going, I mean, do you want to go, um, er, eat this now?"

Shawna's eyebrow lifted, "Rusty, what?"

He tried again, "Um, Shawna, you know how I used to work at Sonic? Well, when I started here, I got a bonus. I have some extra money. I want to spend it on you."

Her eyes widened. Rusty blushed again. "I mean, I want to take you out. To the school dance. I'll get a tux. And flowers. I'll get you flowers." He spread mustard over the back of his hand.

Shawna reached across the counter and touched his cheek. "Really?" She saw him nod and said softly, "I'd like that." He wrapped his hand in white paper and stuck it out to her. The sandwich soaked up pickle juice on the counter.

# Chapter 3

Mary Nell pondered her granddaughter who was curled around the cat, Roberta, humming and tapping the toes of her tap shoes together. Today Bitsy had on a feather boa and a tutu. Mary Nell looked at this outfit in dismay and remembered her conversation with Betty when she had dropped Bitsy off for the day.

Mary Nell had told Betty, "I simply have no idea how I got such a grandchild. Of course, I raised only boys, but I don't understand how this old bra-burner got this little girly-girl that always smells like bubblegum and lollipops."

Betty curved the corner of her mouth upward as she turned to go to the door, "Oh, you'll figure it out. See you around seven."

Now still lost in reverie she heard a little voice interrupt her thoughts, "Grandmary?"

"Hmm?"

"Grandmary, do you think I can be a star?"

Now fully alert, Mary Nell leaned toward Bitsy, "You mean up in the sky?"

"Naw, silly. A dancing star."

"Oh. Well, I think you could be a star if that's what you want badly enough to work for it."

"That's what I thought." She settled back into the swing and bounced one foot up and down as she hummed and stroked Roberta. Then suddenly still, she looked at her grandmother and said, "Grandmary, my name's not really Bitsy."

"I know. Your name is Elizabeth Alice."

"I don't want to be called Bitsy any more."

"OK. Do you like Liz or Lisa or Liza or Beth?" Bitsy's head shook with each name.

"No Grandmary, I want my name to be something I really love. I want my star name to be Pink."

Mary Nell sputtered and got out of her chair to walk to the door, her back now to Bitsy. "Pink? You want me to call you Pink?" Bitsy nodded as Mary Nell's chest shook. She was saved from an outright chortle by the arrival of Lulu and Buck.

"Honey, Lulu would love for you to play ball with her," Mary Nell called as she walked out to meet them.

Buck said he wondered if Walter needed him this afternoon. Bitsy stared at him as she picked up a ball to throw. She closed her brown eye and squinted through her blue eye, looking hard at him.

"Mary Nell, why does she do that?" he squirmed under the scrutiny.

Mary Nell shrugged. "Oh, Walter taught her that. He said looking through blue eyes gave you a clearer view of the world." She paused, batting her very blue eyes, "I don't have a choice."

Bitsy continued to stare at Buck and finally asked, "Is a bull's foot shaped like a moon?"

"Yeah, guess it is."

Walter walked out the door, interrupting the conversation, and he and Buck chatted while Bitsy and Lulu played ball. Buck waved as he walked toward home leaving Lulu to play with Bitsy.

Walter and Mary Nell stood and watched Bitsy for a few moments, then Mary Nell said softly to Walter, "Bitsy wants to change her name. She wants us to call her by her 'star name.'" She nearly strangled trying not to laugh, "She wants to change her name to Pink."

Walter's eyes widened, then he snorted, "Pink. She wants to be Pink. Oh, my God. Pink Floyd." Walter began playing air guitar, "Ba-da-da bum bum bum boo doo. Ba-da-da bum bum bum boo doo." Mary Nell joined in, "Money, get away. Get a good job with more pay and you're okay."

~~~

*"Rusty McCann ordered flowers from Agee's."*

*"He's takin' that Taylor girl to Fall Festival."*

*"Stupid name, Fall Festival. What happened to Homecoming?"*

*"Oh, that's later. They cooked up a new occasion to spend a lot of money."*

Rusty's jitters were getting on everyone else's nerves. "God, Rusty, it's just a school dance. You're not meeting the queen," Betty snapped after he asked for the fourth time if he looked okay. This brother of hers could barely speak to her for looking at himself in the mirror behind her. And his cologne had begun to bother her – it smelled like he'd used half a bottle.

He did look nice, though, she thought, studying the red hair he'd let grow out and had had styled. Its russet tones were highlighted by the bronze tie and cummerbund of his rented tuxedo. He'd said that Shawna's dress was a copper color, and he wanted to look good standing beside her.

He would: he was a good-looking boy. Betty proudly patted him on the shoulder, "You clean up good. You and Shawna will be the 'purtiest' couple at the dance."

A flush spread across Rusty's cheeks. "Aw, sis," he mumbled as he picked up her car keys. "Thanks for lending me your car. I just couldn't drive Dad's truck." He headed out the door, looked back and said with a grin, "I know. I'll be careful. And have a good time. And not stay out too late. Bye."

She watched him open the door to her car, and stumble over a piece of gravel in the road as he tried to get into the front seat. "Please, God, just don't let him fall down!" She sighed and yelled into the kitchen for a missing order of French fries.

Rusty drove slowly to Shawna's house, sneaking looks in the rearview mirror to make sure that the pimple he thought he saw on the side of his nose hadn't popped out in its full red glory yet. He repeated to himself his recent mantra, "It's okay. I'll be okay. It's okay. I'll be okay."

When Shawna came to the door, he couldn't speak. There she stood. Her copper-colored dress matched the highlights in the auburn hair that curled around her bare shoulders. Freckles sprinkled across her nose. A chipped front tooth and a crooked smile accompanied a good-humored sparkle in her dark brown eyes. Her ankles, used to running shoes, wobbled in her high heels.

To Rusty she looked like a goddess. He stared, caught a faint whiff of something spicy, and sniffed. Finally, feeling foolish, he said, "Ah, em. Gosh! Shawna, you smell beautiful!" The familiar heat climbed his neck. "Flowers. I have flowers. Here." He thrust the small white box at her.

Shawna took the florist box, opened it, and smiled at Rusty. "Oh, they're perfect." She pinned the corsage of mums and daisies onto her dress as Rusty looked on, helpless. "Thank you, Rusty. I love them."

Just then the little bouquet made a dive for the floor, and Rusty grabbed at it. He jabbed his thumb on its long straight pin, jerked his hand backward as the corsage tumbled to the floor. "Damn!" he cried, picking up the flowers with one hand while popping his stabbed thumb into his mouth. "Oh, oh, I'm so sorry, Shawna." The blush on his neck and cheeks deepened several shades as he stood in limbo, not knowing what Shawna might do.

She took the flowers from him and looked into his face. "Your eyes get even greener when you're blushing." She re-pinned the corsage, "OK. Let's go."

The drive to the dance was quiet. Very quiet. Rusty couldn't trust himself to say anything. He managed to arrive safely, park the car, open the door, and walk Shawna into the gym.

At the punchbowl, Rusty waited for the server to hand him two glasses, afraid to try to serve himself. He so desperately wanted not to spill something tonight. "I'm okay. I'll be okay," he mumbled. He carried the punch successfully to Shawna, took a sip and carefully planted it on a nearby table. He couldn't trust himself to hold the punch and talk, but he couldn't think of anything to say, so he looked around at the gym decorated in Fall Finery, his toe tapping to the beat of Kenny Chesney's "Boys of Fall".

Finally Shawna set down her glass and took his hand. "Let's dance."

His flush crept back up his neck, hitting his ears on its way to his cheeks as he thought about touching her shoulders. But he managed to get out on the dance floor, take her hand and lead her into a smooth two-step. Shawna was surprised at how well he danced. They made a well-matched team. Other dancers began to notice, and left space around them for their apparently well-practiced routine.

Rusty was oblivious to everything but Shawna and dancing. He liked to dance, and with Shawna in his arms, he felt invincible.

They were still dancing when the lights came on to signal the end of the night's music. Rusty felt an elbow in his side, and turned to see his buddy Jason leaning toward him to whisper, "Hey. I didn't know you could dance like that."

"Yeah. Betty used to make me dance with her. She'd pinch me when I messed up," he whispered back.

"Why don't you all come out to Floyd's Corners with us? We're doing a bonfire."

Rusty nodded then turned back to Shawna, "You ready to leave?"

They took their time walking hand-in-hand out of the school building and to the car. They drove in silence to Floyd's Corners, a few miles outside of town. Cars were already parked along an open field and people were gathered around a nicely burning fire. Smoke drifted upward, smelling like autumn to Rusty.

Jason shoved a beer at Rusty, "Drink up!" Rusty reached to take it, then drew back his hand when the sound of a siren pierced the chatter of the crowd. Jason sprinted back to his cooler, grabbed it by its handle and dragged it toward his old truck.

Rusty grabbed Shawna's hand and started toward Betty's car. "Sorry. Sorry. Sorry." he repeated as they found the car. He opened the door for Shawna then rounded the front of the car just as blue lights hit his face. He tried to duck, but he was spotted.

"What are you kids doing? Trying to set the woods on fire?" Sheriff Jones yelled. "Rusty McCann, is that you? What are you doing out here?" he said, surprised at seeing Betty Floyd's younger brother all spiffed up, with a girl, and in his sister's car.

Rusty mumbled, "Just having a bonfire, sir," then tucked himself into the car, started it, popped it into gear and drove away, heart pounding. They drove in silence to Shawna's house with Rusty trying to think of something to say more original than "I'm sorry about the bonfire. Thank you for a lovely time". When he walked her to her door, he started to say his lines, but she pre-empted him with a soft "Shhh" as she kissed him on the lips.

She opened her door, and he dashed to the car, missed the curb and crashed into the rear fender. He straightened his tux, stood up and mistakenly got into the back seat. After he saw her turn off the porch light, he climbed over the seat, started the car and let out a wild whoop, "Hot Damn!"

# Chapter 4

The next morning, Sheriff Jones walked across the field at Floyd's Corners, looking at the beer cans and trash scattered around the burned circle where the fire had been. He heard a snorting sound and looked up into the blank stare of a large black bull.

There was something decidedly odd about that bull. He stared at nothing, taking no notice of the sheriff or his waving arms as he tried to get the bull's attention. The bull only moved to put his nose in the air and snuffle again.

Something nibbled at the edge of Sheriff Jones' consciousness. That bull just wasn't right. Maybe he'd stop by and warn Walter Floyd to check on his bull.

~~~

A low growl shifted Buck's attention to the sound of tires on his gravel driveway. He glanced up from his game of catch with Lulu. "Walter Floyd. Wonder what he wants, girl." He walked onto the porch. Lulu carried the ball beside him, then tried to bury it in a chair cushion as Buck rocked back and forth on his heels.

Walter's pickup slowed to a stop. He leaned out the window, "Hey, Buck. Just wanted to thank you for noticing that problem with Toro. The sheriff saw it too, so we took a walk through the pasture and found a patch of hemp. And a lot of funny-colored bull crap. Looks like Toro ate a lot of it. No wonder he didn't care about you and Lulu. I can't figger how that patch got started out there. Odd. Anyway, thanks again." He nodded, turned the truck around and drove off. Bitsy's small hand waved out the window as she called, "Bye, Lulu!"

~~~

Mary Nell was quite happily stretched out in her favorite spot. She guessed she'd have called it her "secret hiding place" when she was a kid, but now it was just her resting place. Probably not her final one.

She lay there in the shade of the small grove of trees. She didn't have to do anything or go anywhere. She could just be. There. With the breeze and the soft grass and the blue sky. It had been years since she'd felt so relaxed.

Her mind flicked between memories and current concerns. But none of them seemed very important. Funny how that musty smell in the old jewelry bag she found led her to dig through it in earnest. And sprinkling those old seeds in the pasture was such a lark. She smiled as she thought about the unlikelihood of it all.

She leaned her chin on her hand and was intently watching a bee on a clover blossom when a noise jarred her from her daydream. Mary Nell might be in her mid-fifties, but there was nothing wrong with her hearing. She heard the crunch of tires on gravel well before she could see Walter's truck pull out of Buck's driveway and onto their paved road. It gave her time to walk back up to the house to see what Walter was up to.

Walter thumped the horn twice. Mary Nell walked around from the back of the house and said, "What you want, old man?" Her fondness for Walter softened her tone until it sounded like a caress to him.

"I'm heading to town. Want anything or want to go?"

"No, thanks." She spotted Bitsy, and walked toward her open window. "Hey, Bits!" She leaned in and kissed Bitsy on the top of the head.

Bitsy squirmed around to look at her grandmother. "'Pink,' Grandmary. Remember? Hey, you smell good. Like woods and dirt."

Mary Nell smiled as she leaned further inside the window and patted Walter on the shoulder. "Be back by six, okay? You all be careful." Walter drove away, leaving Mary Nell smiling after him. Big, solid, comfortable Walter with his thinning hair and contagious smile—he was still the nicest man she knew.

Walter thought she smelled good, too. What was that scent? It reminded him of when he first met Mary Nell. She always used to smell like that. What did she call it? Pahjooly?

He began to hum absently as he mused. Hemp in the pasture. How did that happen? Walter hadn't heard of anyone growing hemp around there for 40 years. Back in the early '70s some of those kids on that commune over in Hasselboro were trying to grow it, to make rope they said. The sheriff didn't believe them and burned their fields. Yep, everybody in the path of that smoke slept good that night.

Wasn't Mary Nell friends with some of those kids?

So where did that patch come from? Could seed be dormant for 40 years?

Suddenly Walter realized that Bitsy was singing along with his humming. "Puff the Magic Dragon, Lived by the Sea." "Well, I'll be damned!" he joined her with "And frolicked in the autumn mist in a land called Honah Lee."

# Chapter 5

*"It's nice to have a café in town again."*

*"That Betty works hard. Nice girl."*

*"Hope she doesn't run to fat, like her dad."*

*"Now that Rusty quit football, he'd better watch it, too."*

*"Nothin' worse that football muscle turned to flab."*

Betty chalked "Today's Specials" onto the blackboard at the front of her café. She'd found some tart apples at the farmer's market that she was making into a sauce for the pork loin she'd picked up at the butcher's this morning.

She looked around the café with satisfaction. The black and white checkerboard floor, the chrome-legged tables and chairs, and the stools at the counter had just the friendly old diner look she wanted. She thought she'd done well since Dub left, by buying and fixing up the Main Street Café. It had been hard to swallow her pride and ask Walter for a loan, but he was so nice about it, she came away feeling good about herself and her decision to start her own business.

Her dad would have liked to help her, she knew, but his lack of money and stamina got in the way of most of his good intentions. He was more useless about fixing things than Rusty. And Rusty was just a kid. Old Tommy McCann did only one thing really well – eat. Since Betty's mother died, he'd done little but practice.

Betty took over keeping house and cooking after her mother got sick. He had eaten everything she cooked, praising it loudly. She was a naturally good cook who got even better under the glow of his praise.

Unfortunately, Tommy McCann didn't seem to have an off-switch when it came to food. During Betty's high school years, he gained 147 pounds. As his bulk increased, his mobility decreased until moving from bed to table to recliner became the extent of his daily exercise.

When the doctor told Tommy he needed to lose weight or lose everything, Betty began to cook a healthier diet for her dad. The skills and recipes she built caring for her dad translated into a reputation for healthy, locally grown foods served at her café. Her food was getting attention from health-conscious diners as well as the good-ole-boy friends of her father. As her tables filled, so did her till, and she'd begun to pay back her loan from Walter.

The carrot-colored hair that earned Rusty his nickname was darker and richer on Betty. She was nearly as tall as her brother and nearly as athletic. She used to be good at doubles tennis when she and Dub played, but she'd had little time for anything lately but Bitsy and the café.

Rusty jangled the bell on the door to the café before jauntily walking to the counter. Betty studied him. "Did you and Shawna have a good time at the dance?" she asked as she set a bowl for cereal, a glass for orange juice, and a plate for toast in front of him.

The grin spread from ear to ear. "It was okay", he mumbled reaching for his empty glass.

Betty was busy waiting on other customers as Rusty ate his breakfast. He counted out two dollars and some change and laid them beside his bowl before getting up to leave. Betty looked up at him, starting to say something, but he interrupted, "I'm no mooch."

~~~

*"Wonder what happened to Dub Floyd?"*

*"I heard he moved up to Chicago."*

*"He got him another woman, I bet."*

*"Yeah, someone with skinny parents."*

*"Shh."*

Mary Nell stood on her porch and looked toward the little tenant house where Buck lived. She was glad Walter had hired Buck. He was good with the animals, a quiet neighbor, and not bad on the eyes. She just might pay him a visit. See what kind of housekeeper he was.

As she walked, she let her mind wander from the pleasant weather to the fall color staining the maple leaves to Betty. Too bad Betty had no interest in Buck. Oh, she knew that folks wouldn't understand how she could encourage Betty to look at someone besides Dub. But even if he was her son, he wasn't coming back, and she thought Betty needed to look for adult company elsewhere than at Walter Andrew Floyd, Jr.

Walter didn't like her to think that way. He still dreamed of Dub moving back from Chicago, Dub and Betty getting back together, and Dub taking over the management of the farm and business. But it just wasn't going to happen, Mary Nell was certain. Too much water had flowed under that danged bridge.

~~~

Lulu brought a box turtle into the living room and barked for Buck to play with her. He retrieved the turtle, saying "Silly" as he did so. She cocked her head, pricked her ears, and tried to understand why Buck put the turtle outside. She tilted her head to the other side and let out a slight whine.

"Girl, sure wish others would try so hard to understand me." She looked expectantly as he pitched her favorite yellow tennis ball out the front window where it bounced on the porch rail and into the small front yard. Only seconds behind it, Lulu leaped out the window and across the railing, catching the ball on its first bounce.

"You leap straight up. Look like a deer." Lulu was back with the ball before Buck noticed. She growled and stood with her feet on the window sill. Then her tail wagged as she whined a little and leaped out the window again. Somebody she knows, thought Buck, leaning to look out the window himself.

Mary Nell waved as she saw Buck in the window. "I'm just out for a walk. Thought I'd stop by and say 'howdy!'" She whistled through her teeth, and Lulu magically appeared next to her. She startled, then reached down to pat Lulu's head and looked up at Buck. "Have you trained her to do that? That disembodied movement? She should work for a spiritualist."

"No, ma'am. But she can sure move cattle 'n' sheep. Didn't train her to do that neither. She just does it." Buck looked affectionately at Lulu then back up at Mary Nell. "Help you with anything?"

Mary Nell shook her head, "No, thanks. Just wanted to move my legs this mornin'. I've been sittin' too much lately. I'm gettin' wider by the day." She patted her butt and smiled ruefully. Buck chuckled as Lulu took the pat for an invitation and jumped up against Mary Nell's thigh. Mary Nell scrubbed the top of Lulu's head with her knuckles, then said, "That'll do," quietly. Lulu dropped to the ground.

Buck's eyes widened, "You herd?"

"I have. Had about twenty dog-broke sheep that I used to take to trials. And ran my own dogs. I had a sweet little bitch, Gem, that won a few meets. After she got too old, I kinda lost interest. Reminded me too much of her and how good she was."

Buck nodded. "Felt that way about a horse once. Best ropin' horse I ever knew. After he got hurt, I lost my taste for it. Stuck to bull ridin'. Hard to get attached to a bull."

"In lots of ways," Mary Nell chuckled.

"Speaking of bulls, any news about Toro?"

Mary Nell pulled her eyebrows together. "Hmm? I don't know anything about that big damned bull except he's a mean somethin' and costs a fortune to keep. Why do you ask? Did you hear something?"

"Walter stopped by and said somethin' about hemp. He found some growin' in Toro's pasture and thought Toro ate some."

"Well, he didn't say anything to me. Hemp, huh?"

Buck nodded, Mary Nell shrugged then took the ball Lulu shoved into her leg and threw it. Lulu dashed after it, making a wide outrun before leaping into the air to catch it on the bounce. "Nice dog."

Buck nodded again. "Yep."

"I'd like to see her work cattle sometime. Let me know when you take her out, would ya?" She turned to walk back down the drive. She hadn't thought about herding in a long time. She glanced back over her shoulder at Buck and Lulu. "Nice dog."

Ambling up the drive to the top of the hill, she caught sight of a large patch of dirt. A rectangular plot of recently tilled soil was barely visible beyond the stand of trees at the road's edge. As she stood there thinking, she saw first Lulu then Buck walk from his house, through the woods, and into the open field. Buck carried a brown bag. He carefully reached into it, took something out and scattered it in one corner of the tilled plot. He motioned for Lulu to move away from him and out onto the grass.

Mary Nell walked quickly toward home rehearsing a conversation with Walter as she went. She didn't know what the hell was going on but she meant to find out.

~~~

Rusty drove Betty's car to take Bitsy to Mary Nell for the afternoon. He hoped to sneak in a visit to Shawna before he took the car back. He hadn't seen her except at school since the dance. He wanted to take her out for a Coke, maybe. Or a coffee. He wondered if she drank coffee. She probably did. Lattes, he bet. With sugar.

"Uncle Rusty?" Bitsy interrupted his thoughts. "What's Mr. Buck doin' over there? See? Through the trees? Lulu's with him. What's he doin'?"

Rusty slowed and looked the where Bitsy pointed. "Don't know, Bits. I can't quite see him. Looks like he's pulling some brush out of the woods."

"Why's he doin' that?"

"Don't know. Maybe he's gonna burn it."

"Why'd he wanna burn it? He might get in trouble."

"Who'd he get in trouble with?"

"Maybe with Grandmary. She says we shouldn't set fires."

Rusty glanced at Bitsy, not sure how to respond. Finally he shrugged and said, "Why don't you sing me a song while we drive up to Grandmary's."

Bitsy pursed her lips and tapped them with a forefinger. She began to hum, making woo-woo sounds as she continued to tap her lips. Then she sang to a never-before-heard tune, "Lulu is runnin'. Lulu is runnin'. Lulu is a-runnin'. Bark, bark, bark. Mr. Buck is draggin' a tree but Lulu is a-runnin'…."

~~~

After he dropped Bitsy off, Rusty headed back into town. He slowed as he neared the spot where Bitsy had seen Buck and Lulu. Buck was still in the field, and it looked like he was dragging a dead bush over a muddy spot. What the heck was he up to? Rusty watched a few minutes longer, looking for but not finding Lulu. Weird.

He then sped up, grinned, as he thought about seeing Shawna again. The next thing he was aware of was the stop sign at the corner of Shawna's street. He pulled in front of her house and had a talk with himself before getting out. "It'll be okay if she's not there. It'll be okay if she's busy. I'm okay. I'll be okay."

He knocked on the door and shuffled from foot to foot waiting. Then there she was. The sun touched the top of her head when she opened the door and he thought he was in the presence of glory. Surely an angel could be no more beautiful. He remembered the shepherds in the field being struck dumb, sore afraid, when they saw an angel. He hoped he could speak. "Oh, God, let me speak," he silently prayed.

"Hey, Shawna," he finally managed. "Do you want to go get a Coke or a coffee?"

She glanced down at herself – overlarge t-shirt stained on one sleeve and baggy-kneed jeans worn at least one day too long. "Uh. I guess. Yes. But look at me. I can't go out like this."

Rusty blinked in astonishment. He'd been looking at her. It was about all he could do. And she looked, sigh, wonderful. He roused himself to say, "No. I mean, yes. I mean, you look fine. Great. You, um, we could go to a drive-in and stay in the car. You're fine. More. Better. Uh, can you go? I mean, will you?"

Shawna looked at Rusty and thought of her niece who was trying to learn to ride a bike. *Wobbles*, that was it. Rusty had wobbles. She hoped he'd get his balance soon. It was hard on him despite it being cute.

"OK, Rusty. If we don't have to get out of the car. And I have to be home by 5:30 to help with supper. OK? Let me tell my mom."

Rusty couldn't stop nodding. She'd go! He waited on the stoop, clinging with one hand to the wrought-iron rail that extended from the steps to the door. Then he leaned against the doorframe, inadvertently ringing the doorbell. He startled, and jumped back just as Shawna appeared. She was about to scold him for his impatience when she realized what must have happened. Wobbles.

They drove to the local Sonic where Rusty knew everyone since he had worked there until recently. "Hey, Rusty," said the girl who came out to bring their order. "I 'bout didn't recognize you in this car." She stuck her head into the open window and said, "Hey, Shawna." She smirked as she took the money from Rusty after depositing a Coke and a cherry limeade on the window-borne tray. She walked away, swaying her hips and looking back over her shoulder to flash a smart-ass grin.

Shawna was amused. Little Melody Moody was flirting with Rusty, and he was oblivious. She leaned across him to retrieve her limeade just as he turned toward her to ask her if she wanted a straw. They bumped faces.

"God, how could I be so clumsy?" Rusty muttered as Shawna kissed him on the cheek. He was so cute when he wobbled.

They managed to drink their drinks, discuss the football game, and speculate about the contents of tomorrow's math quiz before Shawna said that she needed to get home. Rusty drove carefully, parked competently, and walked her to the door. He leaned over her shoulder to open the storm door for her and kissed her hair lightly as she went inside. "Bye, Rusty. Thanks," she said softly.

But he was already half-way back to the car, a big grin lighting up his freckled face. Maybe he'd have a date to Homecoming after all. If he could figure out how to ask her.

When he returned the keys to Betty, Rusty noticed that The Ladies Corner was empty. Bonnie, Madge, Stella, and Doris, who had been there earlier, had gone home to monitor kids and get supper.

Everyone called them "The Ladies" but Mary Nell called them a "Greek Chorus". She said they were always commenting on everything but were not major players. He wasn't sure exactly what she meant, but he did know that these women could talk – about everybody and everything in the county. If you wanted to know anything, all you had to do was sit near them during their weekly "tea party" at their favorite booth, The Ladies Corner.

He guessed Betty put up with their small orders and long table-time for their entertainment value. "Did The Ladies say anything good today?"

"I don't really know. The Reese's Pieces were here and I didn't have time to listen."

Rusty's eyes danced. He'd named the Reese family's six children "Reese's Pieces" and Betty had picked it up. Those kids were a handful. Two sets of twins, a six year old and a baby. All A's: the two-year old twins were Annie and Amy; the four-year olds were a mixed pair, Alice and Alex; Amber was the oldest; and Amos the baby. He wondered if the Reese parents knew how to stop.

Rusty looked from The Ladies Corner to Betty. "Charlie will let you know if it was juicy."

Betty nodded. Charlie Keller made it a point to sit at the booth next to The Ladies every week. He spent many afternoons at the café since his wife passed. Betty didn't mind. He left good tips, and he was a good news source.

"Whew! Where did you take Shawna this afternoon?"

Rusty's eyes widened in surprise. "How'd you know I saw Shawna?"

"I've got a nose, don't I? You smell way too 'purty' not to have seen Shawna."

"God, Betty." He turned to leave, then paused, "I'll take Bits out to Mary Nell's tomorrow, too, if you want."

"Sure you've got enough cologne?"

Rusty flipped her off as he walked through the door.

~~~

*"Mary Nell Floyd seems kinda restless since she quit workin'"*

*"Bet she's glad not to have to go to all them foreign places, tellin' them how to do stuff."*

*"I never did understand what that company she worked for did. Were they a movin' company?"*

*"Naw. They figgered out how to schedule stuff. Get things from one place to another. Transport."*

*"Fancy name for movin', I'm thinkin'."*

The tilled soil down by the tenant house started Mary Nell to think about growing things. She thought she'd like to have a small greenhouse. She loved having greens in the winter and thought there was no reason that an intelligent woman couldn't build a structure sturdy enough to support plastic.

First, though, she had to locate some tools. She knew where a hammer and a couple of screwdrivers were. She kept them in a drawer in the kitchen. But she thought those wouldn't be enough. Oh, dang, here she was putting last things first again. She didn't even have any plans, and she was trying to gather up tools.

She sat down at the kitchen table with her laptop, a pad and a pencil. She thought she could Google "greenhouse plans" and see if she could find anything that would work. And if she was lucky, there'd even be a list of materials and tools she'd need.

She had barely begun scanning the search results when Bitsy came running into the house. "Grandmary, I'm here! Where are you?"

"In the kitchen, honey." She thought of all the projects she'd planned to do since she retired from the corporate crap, but none of them had been completed. Seemed like there was always somebody overriding something she planned to do. Oh, well, an afternoon with her granddaughter was always a joy. She could make lists later.

"What's up, buttercup?" Mary Nell chirped to Bitsy. The endearment was a natural – Bitsy was clothed all in bright yellow, from tennis shoes to slicker. That child certainly had a flair for costume! "Why don't you take off your jacket? You'll get too warm."

"Oh, I can't, Grandmary. I need it for the play." Bitsy spread open the bottom of the slicker wide as she dipped into a deep curtsy.

"What play, Bits? I don't know anything about a play."

"Well, Grandmary. We haven't wrote it yet. You and me have to write it and then do it for Gramps. And maybe Mamma."

"Oh, I see. Well, I have a pad and pencil right here. Let's start writing."

Bitsy rolled her eyes. "Grandmary, you *know* we have to have our milk and cookies first."

Mary Nell got up, gave Bitsy a hug, and walked to the fridge. "White or brown?" she said holding out a carton of milk in each hand.

Bitsy cocked her head, "What kind of cookies?"

"Lemon or ginger."

"Hmm. I guess white and lemon. Oooor, brown and lem—no, that'd be bad. Mmm, brown and ginger'd be good."

She pointed to her left "White and lemon," then to her right, "Brown and ginger." Then pointing first left then right, "Eeenie, meenie, miney, moe." She stopped, made smoothing motions with her hands, then pointed first right then left, "Eeenie, meenie, miney, moe. I choose you!" She pointed to the left, "White and lemon, Grandmary. Please."

Mary Nell looked on in amazement. Her arms had gotten tired from holding out the cartons of milk so she had set them on the counter. Now, shaking her head, she put the chocolate milk away and got out the lemon cookies. Everything with Bitsy was a drama.

"Bitsy, I have an idea. Maybe the play could be about choosing your snack. You could do "eeenie meenie" and I could bring it to you."

"Oh, Grandmary," Bitsy sighed. "That's boring. But I will need more lemon cookies to match." She took a bite from one of the cookies.

"Match what?"

"Me. I'm yellow. The play will be about yellow. I'll sing a yellow song. And you can bring me a banana." She twirled around the kitchen as she spoke.

"OK. I've got some bananas. But do you know a yellow song?"

"Sure." She did a series of complicated tap steps then stopped and began singing, "We all live in a yellow superbean, yellow superbean, yellow superbean." She waved her hand as if conducting.

"Bits, it's *submarine*. It's a boat that goes under the ocean."

"Well, I don't WANT to go under the ocean." She jumped up, spun around, tapped her toes and heels. Then she stopped, put her hands on her hips, and flounced toward Mary Nell, "Now, Grandmary, you bring me the banana." She resumed tapping, "Yellow superbean. Yellow superbean."

After Bitsy went home, Mary Nell sat back down at her laptop. She sighed remembering Bitsy's "play" performed for Walter and Betty, with the supporting role of banana-hander played by herself. That child was a trip. A real trip.

She looked at a set of building plans on the screen of her laptop. Hmmm. Wonder what else she could grow in that greenhouse.

# Chapter 6

The next afternoon, Betty was sitting at a booth doodling on an order pad when Walter dropped in for a cup of coffee. "Why so glum, Betty?" he said, winking at her.

She looked up, smiled slightly, and said, "Oh, I'm trying to come up with a new promotion. I'm thinking about doing a "Last Meal" contest that for twenty dollars lets you enter the menu you'd want for your last meal on earth. Then I'd have a drawing and cook a special dinner using the winning menu. It would promote my café, and I'd give the entry fees to charity. Whadaya think?"

"Last Meal sounds kinda grim," he replied. "How about Dream Dinner?"

"Yeah. That's good."

"Would you have to have more than one thing on your menu?"

"Uh-huh. I was thinking of a seven-course meal. Soup to nuts."

Walter nodded, "OK. I could enter. I know what I'd want."

"Really? That fast? OK, what would you want?"

"Cheeseburger." He paused, "Seven of 'em."

Betty hooted. "If you win, you got 'em. You're wonderful, Walter," she reached across the table and squeezed his hand.

Walter looked pleased, then glanced away. "Where's my little princess?" he said, looking in the opposite direction from where Bitsy sat on the floor drawing on a piece of paper.

"Gramps, I'm right here! Can't you see anymore?" Bitsy jumped up and threw herself onto her grandfather's lap. "Do you need glasses? Or maybe you need a dog. I bet Lulu could help you."

"No honey, I'm okay. I don't need a dog. Besides, a dog couldn't tell me what you're drawing on that paper."

"Oh, Gramps! I'm drawing a green house for Grandmary. She said she wanted one. I don't know why, though. I think your yellow house is real purty. But will you take it to her?" She placed the paper in front of him.

"Sure will, sweet pea. See ya later, alligator." Walter picked up the drawing, tucked it under his arm, and ruffled Bitsy's hair on his way out the door.

Outside, he glanced again at the drawing of the "green house" Bitsy had made. Well, it *was* green. But Mary Nell wanted a greenhouse? Whatever for? She'd never grown anything in her life.

Betty was still chuckling over Walter's menu suggestion when Buck strolled in. He nodded and sat at the counter, looking over the menu.

Betty walked behind the counter to take his order. She was waitressing alone today since her part-timer had quit to get married. She had to hire more help. At least it wasn't too busy for her to keep up with. Though that was a mixed blessing – no business, no money.

"Haven't seen much of you lately. Walter been keepin' you busy? What can I get you?" she asked as she lay down napkin and silverware in front of him.

"Cheeseburger," he said, nodding.

A loud clap of laughter from Betty caused Buck to eye her with concern. She recovered from her explosion then said with a big grin, "I'm sorry, but Walter was just here, and," she dissolved into another spasm of giggles. Finally catching her breath, she said, "Sorry. Let me get your order going and then I'll start from the beginning."

After hearing of Walter's menu, Buck, too, laughed. "OK, you're forgiven."

Betty glanced over at him with an appraising look. "So, Buck, how about you? Would you pay twenty dollars to enter my contest for a chance to win your dream dinner?"

"Heck, yeah. But you'd be hard pressed to fix it, this time of year."

Her brow wrinkled as she asked, "Why? Something really seasonal? I can get almost anything from the food broker."

"Hey, you're not gonna get my secret menu out of me until the contest. Might give you too many ideas." He grinned and took a sip of the Coke she'd delivered.

She sniffed, then went to the window for his order. "Cheeseburger for the smart ass," she said, placing it in front of him. One corner of her mouth remained up-turned as she returned to her table. She began writing in her notebook, saying slowly as she did so, "Rule number three, no smart asses."

~~~

Rusty walked into his house with dragging feet. It wasn't that he didn't love his dad. He did. But he hated to see him slowly killing himself with his eating. And he'd gotten so big he couldn't do anything, go anywhere. Rusty exhaled heavily as he opened the door, expecting to see his father squeezed into his recliner, munching on something, as usual.

Those munchies. Where did he get them? Rusty sure didn't buy them. And he knew Betty didn't. But his dad always had some hidden away somewhere. Who was his supplier? Somebody had to bring them out here. His dad sure as heck didn't get them himself.

Walking into the living room, Rusty looked startled. His dad wasn't there. He called out, "Dad, I'm home." No reply. He looked in the kitchen, bathroom, bedrooms. Heck, he even looked in the closet, saying under his breath, "As if he could be in here."

He went out the back door to the shed. His dad hadn't been out there in years, but while he was looking…. No. There was no way he could even get in the door. Crap was stacked four-foot high. Yeah, he remembered leaving it that way when his dad had fussed at him to put the Christmas ornaments up last summer. He'd just shoved them in. What a mess! And it smelled like cat pee. God, somebody really needed to clean out this junk hole. And if were going to get done, God knows he'd have to do it.

Where the hell was his dad? He walked behind the shed, back around to the front of the house, and out into the road. Hands on hips, he looked up and down the road. Nothing. Now beginning to worry, he walked back through the house, looking again in every room. Nothing.

He flopped down on the couch, picked up the phone and hit "1" on the speed dial.

"Main Street Café," Betty answered. Her phone voice was so pleasant it calmed him down some.

"Betty, Dad's not home. Do you know where he is?"

"Not home? Dad's not home? Are you sure you looked?"

"Yes, dammit. I looked. He's not exactly easy to overlook. He's not here. Do you have any idea where he is?" He rubbed his left hand over the side of his head and down his neck as he spoke.

"No, Rusty. I don't know. Do you need me to come out there?" Worry slipped her voice into exasperated-mother mode.

Rusty leaned back against the couch and took a deep breath. "No, you don't need to come out here. I'll handle it," he said in the sing-song voice of a rebellious teenager.

"Sorry. I'm just worried. Let me know when he gets back or if you want me to do anything. OK?"

"OK, bye Betty." Rusty couldn't think of anything to do so he flipped channels until he found a game. At least he could see how the Cowboys were doing.

About half-way through the third quarter, with the Cowboys leading the Chiefs by 24-13, a car Rusty didn't recognize pulled up in the driveway. Tommy McCann got out and waddled to the house, waving to the driver as he did.

When he came inside, Rusty looked him over. He seemed okay. Maybe a little tense. "Where you been?"

"Went out for a while. Had coffee." He rubbed the gray stubble on the side of his head, then down his neck, and pulled at the back of his neck several times.

"Who was that dropped you off?"

"A friend. You don't know 'em. Why the third degree?" Tommy was getting irritated.

"I was worried. You never go anywhere. I thought you might be hurt. Or sick, or somethin'."

"Or somethin'." Tommy opened the refrigerator door, took several deep breaths, closed the door, picked up a glass and filled it with water from the sink. After several swallows, he went back into the living room, looked thoughtfully at Rusty watching TV, and sat in his recliner.

He pulled the handle to raise the feet as he adjusted himself in the chair. "Who's winning?"

"Dallas." Rusty mumbled and left the room, taking the phone with him.

# Chapter 7

Mary Nell's trip to the hardware store was a success. After she'd decided to use the University's plans for a backyard greenhouse, the rest was easy. The free PDF version that she'd downloaded from the internet contained materials and tools lists. "O brave new world, that has such freebies in't," she proclaimed loudly. She chuckled thinking of what Maude Roberts, her high school English teacher and nemesis, would say about that mangling as she unloaded her truck into the big open shed behind the house.

Now she just needed to site her project. She'd read about east-west exposure, not under trees, flat, well-drained, etc. But she was presently more concerned with the view and the feel. The technicalities could come later.

She took the plans with her as she walked to the southwest corner of the mowed area around the house. She thought it might work since it was not too far from the barn where she'd store her tools, and close to the main waterline that ran from the well to the house.

One advantage of having a husband with a construction company was that she could requisition all the heavy equipment she'd need to dig the footings and level and gravel the floor. For that matter, she could get some of the boys to erect the building, but she thought it would be fun to do it herself. Surprise the heck out of Walter, too.

Nudged from her reverie by the beep-beep of a car's horn, she walked back toward the house to see who was honking. The mail carrier stood beside her truck holding a large envelope. "Registered letter," she called to Mary Nell who was nearly to the driveway. Mary Nell nodded and kept walking.

"Whew, I'm out of shape," she panted. "That doesn't look like much of a hill until you try to walk up it quickly." She reached for the clipboard that Myrna held, signed her name, and took the letter. "Thanks," she managed to get out, still breathing quickly.

"No problem. You have a blessed day!" Myrna Tyree was a newly-converted Pentecostal. Or "Holy Roller" as Walter called them. She was always pleasant, but that "Blessed Day" crap tended to make Mary Nell skeptical. Well, that and the fact that she'd known Myrna for about thirty years, and not only knew where her bodies were buried but had helped her closet some of the skeletons that had been dug up over the years.

Oh, well. Maybe that new preacher-husband of Myrna's would change things. Yeah, maybe.

She finally noticed she was still holding the envelope Myrna had delivered. She tore it open wondering what could be so important that someone would spend twelve dollars and forty-three cents to send it to her. She pulled out a letter on heavy ivory bond from a law firm. Someone named Billy J. Yeats wanted to meet with her about a bequest. She flipped the envelope over to see if it was from Nigeria. She'd gotten several of those "Dear Madame" letters that promised immense riches if she'd send a few thousand dollars to settle the estate.

No. This one was from Kansas City. Who did she know in Kansas City? Oh, right. Her grandmother's sister, Aunt Bess. She was very old, but she was still alive. Wasn't she?

~~~

Walter looked up and down Main Street with pride of ownership. No, he didn't own the entire street, but he did have a big chunk of it. After he converted the empty, nearly falling down buildings into clean, inviting spaces, the people leasing those spaces built shops and businesses and offices. And revitalized the town while they were at it.

He loved this little place. Sure it was just a wide place on the highway, but it was becoming something again. Recapturing some of the, well, glory of its previous life. This had once been a prosperous little town with doctors and lawyers and bankers filling the large houses that flanked Main Street and the primary cross-street, Maple.

Walter had bought and refurbished many of those houses, too. And then sold them at attractive terms to professional people who wanted to escape the cities. He'd advertised in some of the "green" magazines, trying to attract a new type of settler to these old Ozark hills.

And he was succeeding: a dentist, a CPA, and a veterinarian, all family members from Tulsa had recently moved around the corner from a family practice physician and her therapist husband from Springfield, Missouri. Folks from Kansas City, St. Louis, and Little Rock were filtering into the neighborhood. The houses had started to show the same signs of life as the business district in Blue Fork, Arkansas.

Betty's Main Street Café was a central part of Walter's overall plan. Her healthy menus had given him the idea to encourage more "green" businesses: local produce; alternative energy sources; a farmer's co-op for organic growing. He was planting all the seeds he could, hoping that some of them would sprout. And it looked like he might have a good crop.

The clean smell of freshly cut wood drifted down the street from the building two doors away. His crew was framing the interior walls for the dressing rooms in the new clothing store. And across the way, the painters were putting a final coat on the exterior trim. It looked and smelled like promise.

While he stood there, admiring all the activity on the street, The Ladies traipsed into Betty's Café. "Good lord, is it 2:00 already?" he thought.

~~~

Charlie Keller had taken up his Wednesday afternoon position at the booth next to The Ladies Corner. He sipped coffee and picked at a piece of pie. He wanted it to last a while since it wouldn't do to look as though he was only there to eavesdrop on The Ladies, even though everyone knew he was.

The new part-time waitress, Terri Scott, had cleaned the table in The Ladies corner and laid it with napkins, silverware and glasses of water. They weren't a demanding bunch, but Betty thought it wise to keep them happy. They were an influential group who always knew everything, commented on everything, and judged everything.

Tall, bleached blonde Stella Huff was the first to come in. Her loud voice and cat eye glasses made her instantly the center of attention. Betty wondered if she and Madge Simon had made up yet. They tended to get involved in their children's arguments, staying angry with each other far longer than the kids did.

Madge was next in the door. Her hair was about the same color as Stella's, but that was their only similarity. She was at least six inches shorter, 50 pounds heavier, and much more imaginative. The play she had written for the neighborhood kids to put on was a hit with kids and parents alike. Bitsy had loved being a Faerie, flitting around in her tutu and tapping her wand.

Bonnie Greene and Doris Parks came in together. As far as Betty knew, they didn't argue with each other, but she would be hard pressed to find a more unlikely set of friends. Bonnie was as wholesome as Doris was sultry. Bonnie's graying dark hair was always too short, too curly, too something. Her nails were broken from digging in the garden, and her clothes looked thrown on rather than planned.

Doris however was hairspray and hair dye, perfume and makeup, nail polish and knife-sharp creases in her stylish khaki pants. Her long dark red hair perfectly curled around her shoulders, even when the gray roots needed touching up. She always wore her clothes a bit too tight, a bit too bright, a bit too young.

Those four were the basis of The Ladies. Two others, Helen Poole and JoAnn Waters sometimes joined them, so Betty always set their table for six. Once they were seated and their orders taken, they fell into their usual habit of non-stop talk.

*"Jack Junior Jones died at the worst possible time. How is anyone going to find time to put on a decent send-off?"*

*"Well, I know I'm busy. I'm workin' with the high school kids to get our 'Rose Bowl Parade' floats ready by next week. And we're out of crape paper. I've been to every Dollar General in three counties."*

*"Brother James told us at the altar guild meeting that he will not allow anything on the pulpit that has anything to do with pumpkins, witches, or turkeys. I've got to come up with a new theme by Sunday. I guess I'll have to drive to Little Rock to the Hobby Lobby. I don't know where I'll find the time. I've got the kids doing a play for Halloween. And the knitting club.... And a funeral?"*

*"Joyce called me to invoke the telephone tree. We've got to get food prep lined out for the week. Casseroles and sandwiches every day. I'll be up all night cookin'"*

*"Helen's Jimmy's only sister. I wonder if she's helping Peggy with the arrangements. They haven't been real friendly since Jack's mom left her new stove to Peggy instead of Helen."*

*"God, girls, you are not going to believe this. I just talked to Helen. She is mortified. I mean it. I don't know if she'll ever get over it."*

*"Why? What happened?"*

*"Peggy called her to talk about the arrangements for Jack Junior. She told Helen that she knows everybody's real busy and she's worried about attendance at the service. She doesn't want the kids to be embarrassed. So she's not going to use Johnson's, even though the Jones always use Johnson's. She's going to Merk's."*

*"Merk's? They're way over on the other side of town."*

*"I know. But that's not all. Merk's has a new building. The old First National Bank branch out on the highway. You can rent it for the viewing. A drive-by viewing. They put the body in the window and the guest book in the slide-out drawer."*

*"Drive-by viewing? Mercy! Can't Helen talk her out of it?"*

*"She said she couldn't even discuss it. She's nearly speechless. Well, for Helen."*

Betty finally got loose from the Reese's Pieces who were ordering a late lunch. She wandered back to The Ladies Corner to see what was causing the uproar. When they saw her approach, they tried to straighten up, but finally JoAnn exploded, "Oh, Betty, you just won't believe this" and they began to tell her all the details. As they always did.

They had just about stopped rehashing the news and were shaking their heads saying "Oh, God" or "Oh, my" when Bitsy ran back to find her mother. "Mamma, where's my Pop Goes the Weasel?"

Betty said, "Bitsy, I've told you to keep track of your toys. I don't know where your Jack in the Box is."

JoAnn sputtered. "Oh, God. A Jack in the Box!" and the cackling returned. As one of the women would get herself under control, another would break out again, until the entire group hugged their aching ribs.

Stella tried to calm the hilarity. "Ladies," she admonished. "We're becoming a spectacle."

Doris looked up with still streaming eyes. "Oh, honey. They ain't seen nothin' yet."

# Chapter 8

Bitsy curled up on Walter's lap after lunch. She needed a nap but was fighting it. "Gramps, tell me a story. You tell 'em good."

Walter patted her back gently and scooted her into a more comfortable position for himself. "OK. What do you want me to tell you about?"

Bitsy laid her head against his shoulder and took his left hand into hers. She played with his fingers and twisted his ring round and round. "Tell me 'bout why something is."

Walter puzzled that out for a minute, then said, "Do you want to hear about why our town is called 'Blue Fork'?"

"Um-hmm." She continued to play with his hand pulling his expandable watch band out and letting it snap back against his wrist. During one pull, the band caught a few hairs. Walter jerked away from her. "Sorry, Gramps. Give it back."

He put his hand back in hers and began to speak, softly and slowly, "A long time ago when people were just beginning to move to this part of the Ozarks, one family built their cabin extra big. Bigger than they needed just for themselves. They thought they could rent out beds to travelers. And sell them some dinner, too. Do you know what places like that are called, Bits?"

"Ummm, Motel 6?"

Walter smiled, "Now they are. But back then they were called 'inns'."

"Like Days Inn?"

"Yep. Only then everybody just called it 'the inn' because it was the only one around. After a while, some other people a few miles away also opened an inn. So now there were two inns and you couldn't just say 'the inn' anymore without getting confused."

"So whad they do?" She was now playing with her hair, wrapping a curl around a finger again and again.

"Well, many people didn't know how to read back then, so just writing something like 'Bitsy's Inn' wouldn't work. So they usually painted things on signs and called the inn by what was in the picture. The inn a few miles away had a big black cat painted on its sign, so people called it 'The Black Cat'."

"Whad they call our inn, Gramps?" Her eyes were at about half-mast and her hair twirling had slowed.

"The owner wanted to do something special because he sold meals along with a place to sleep. So he made a great big spoon and fork and painted them bright blue and hung them up outside his house."

"Whafor?"

"So people could call the inn, 'The Fork and Spoon.' That way they could tell the difference between the two inns. But one time, there was a bad storm with high winds. And it knocked down the big spoon and broke it. The man that owned the inn didn't have time to make a new spoon since he had to plant his fields. So he just left that big old fork hanging on his house. And pretty soon, people called it 'The Blue Fork'."

"More and more people moved to the area, and pretty soon they built up a bunch of houses around that inn. And after a while there was a fire, and the inn burned down. But people still called that area, 'Blue Fork' because that old inn had been there so long. When the people decided to make their settlement a real town, they kept the name. And that's why our town is named Blue Fork."

Walter looked down at the lolling head of his granddaughter. She was asleep, as he expected. He carefully stood shifting her into his arms and carried her to the bedroom. Walking out onto the porch, he saw Mary Nell, curled up on the porch swing, reading. "Hon, do you know where Blue Fork got its name?"

She looked up at him as if he had sprouted horns. "Well, of course. It's from the fork in the river. The main channel ran through a very wooded area and looked nearly black, but this fork ran through a clearing where the sky reflected on the water turning it blue. Why?"

"Oh, just wondering. I put Bitsy down for her nap."

Mary Nell nodded, then returned to her book. Walter was acting decidedly odd. Which reminded her, "Hey, what's going on with your bull? Buck said something about it eating hemp."

"I don't really know. Buck mentioned to me that Toro didn't seem right. Then the sheriff said he thought something was wrong with him. So the sheriff and I went looking, and found a bunch of funny-colored bull crap and some chewed up plants that look like hemp. I don't get it. Where'd hemp come from and how'd it get in the middle of that field?"

"Hmm. Strange."

"Yep."

"Something else strange. I saw a freshly tilled plot over near the tenant house. You doing something over there?"

"No. Don't know anything about it. Where was it?"

"Up the hill from the tenant house. Back from the road. Can't hardly see it. I would have missed it except I caught sight of some movement. Buck and Lulu were up there and it looked like Buck was planting seeds."

Walter screwed up his mouth into a half-frown and shook his head. "Dunno. I'll check on it." He scratched his chin, "When's Betty coming for Bits?"

"She's not. I'm taking her home."

"I'll take her. I need to go to town anyway." And maybe tell Bitsy another version of how Blue Fork got its name.

~~~

*"Walter Floyd's sure good about payin' attention to that Taylor boy."*

*"Yeah. Seems like those girls could use some attention, too."*

Dressed in jeans and a t-shirt, Shawna finished vacuuming the carpet in her bedroom Since her mother had gone back to work part-time, she was expected to help out more around the house. She didn't mind vacuuming, but boy, she hated to dust. She always tried to get her chores done before her sister started so that she could have the pick of the chores.

At seventeen, Shawna was responsible enough to be trusted taking care of her younger sister and brother after school. That allowed her mother to actually bring home some money rather than spend it all on after-school care. Pete and Maisie were pretty good kids. Maisie at thirteen was getting too big for her brightly flowered panties in Shawna's opinion, but Shawna could still win against her in any argument.

Pete was still a little kid at ten, so keeping him happy consisted of feeding him and letting him watch TV or have a friend over to play video games or soldiers or something. Shawna didn't get the attraction of moving toy soldiers around on the floor of the den, but as long as Pete was quiet, she didn't much care.

Since Shawna started dating Rusty, she wanted to spend more time with him. Well, whenever he could get up the nerve to ask her out. But she had to be home the three afternoons a week that her mother worked doing the books for the new veterinarian who'd moved to town. Her mother seemed happier working. She loved animals and really liked Dr Susan Baker who lived in one of the big houses on Maple Street with her dentist sister and her sister's CPA husband.

John Taylor, Shawna's dad, had been killed in an accident at work when a crane malfunctioned and crushed him. Floyd Construction Company's insurance and Walter Floyd himself had taken care of the family ever since. Walter felt guilty for the accident, Shawna knew, although no one blamed him. But he decided that Pete needed some adult male companionship and would frequently take him fishing, camping, or to a ball game. It was good for Pete, Shawna thought. It make him feel important. Walter was a good role model, and a much better companion for Pete than Shawna, her mother, or her sister.

Her sister fishing – that was a laugh. Maisie tried to avoid the great outdoors in every possible way. She seemed perfectly happy to be inside a house, a school, a store or some other building permanently. She had no sense of seasons or weather. Today she was dressed for deep summer in shorts, flip-flops, and a tank top. "Maisie, would you go get the mail," Shawna called from the kitchen where she was making a salad.

Maisie stepped out onto the porch and immediately returned. "It's cold," she chattered.

Shawna looked at her in amazement. It was November outside. "Put some clothes on, for God's sake," she said in exasperation. Maisie was so not together.

Maisie pulled on an old raincoat and dashed out the door without looking, nearly colliding with Rusty who'd just walked up to the house. Both blushed furiously and mumbled apologies. "Shawna," Maisie stuck her head back in the house, "someone's here to see you." She then dashed down the driveway, grabbed the mail from the mailbox, flew back to the porch, pushed past the waiting Rusty with only a nod, and dove into the house.

Shawna came to the door at last, saw Rusty, and stepped outside to talk with him. "Sorry, Rusty, but I can't ask you in. My mom's at work, and I'm not allowed to have boys over when she's not home."

Rusty nodded. "That's okay. I just stopped to ask if you'd like to go to Homecoming with me. I got the day off. We could go to the game, have dinner, and go to the dance. If you want to, I mean."

Shawna was amazed. It was the most consecutive words that Rusty had ever spoken to her. He was getting his balance. "I'd like that. A lot." She smiled sweetly at him.

Rusty nodded again. "OK. See you. Later." He turned, tripped over the doormat, and sprawled down the steps, catching himself on the railing just before landing on his knees. "Oh, Jeez! I am such a klutz!" he mumbled, his face flaming.

Shawna tried to hide her wide grin behind her hand. "Still wobbly." She shook her head and went back inside to her salad.

~~~

Billy J. Yeats, attorney for the estate of Miss Bess Campbell, turned into the road leading to the Floyds' large white frame house. He'd made several attempts to meet with Mary Nell before now. She wasn't an easy one to nail down. Now finally he would tell her the terms of her aunt's will. He knew she'd be surprised by the stipulations placed on the disposition of the estate. He grinned. He liked to surprise people.

Mary Nell saw the skinny bald man approach her house from the car he'd parked in her driveway. He looked like someone wanting something. Mormon or Jehovah's Witness, maybe, or Kirby salesman. But she supposed it was probably that lawyer come down from Kansas City about Aunt Bess's will. He had asked her to go to Kansas City, but she'd been adamant. If he wanted to meet her, he could jolly well come to her. She wasn't at all sure she wanted anything to do with Bess Campbell's estate, anyway.

She remembered very little of Aunt Bess. She was her grandmother's sister, her mother's aunt. She was the oldest, and Grandma was the youngest. Between them was a string of boys. Mary Nell couldn't remember how many. She never knew any of them. War, accidents, and heart attacks killed all of them off before Mary Nell was born. Grandma hadn't been close to her sister. In fact, Mary Nell remembered her being a bit afraid of her. There was some half-heard conversation between her mother and grandmother that was nibbling at the edge of her consciousness.

It was with fairly negative expectations that she opened the door to the Kansas City lawyer. He wasn't what she'd expected in his polyester suit and loud skinny tie. He stuck out his scarecrow arm toward her. "Billy J. Yeats, ma'am. Are you Mary Nell Floyd?"

Mary Nell shook his hand, assured him of her identity, and invited him inside. She offered him coffee or tea, but he declined. He said he wanted to get down to business. "Mrs. Floyd, I've come to apprise you of the contents of Bess Campbell's will," he said, seating himself on the indicated couch.

"Mary Nell, please."

"Mary Nell. Very well. You have been named the primary beneficiary of your aunt. She left some unusual stipulations with her bequest, and it is those stipulations I've come here to tell you about. Are you with me?"

Mary Nell stiffened at his condescension. "I've understood your words, but I have no idea why Aunt Bess would leave me anything. What does her estate entail?"

"I told you there were some odd stipulations. One of them is that you cannot be informed of the extent or content of the estate for thirty days."

"Then why did you come here now?" Mary Nell was becoming irritated with this silliness. "Why didn't you just wait thirty days?"

"No, you misunderstand me. It is thirty days from the time I give you this package." He handed her what looked like an old box of typing paper, yellowed and stained on one side. "I can answer no questions about the contents of this box, nor of the estate, for thirty days. I am certain you will have questions, so shall we set up our next appointment for thirty days from today? I will come here again. Will 2:00 pm be suitable?"

Mary Nell fiddled with the top of the box as he spoke. She looked up at him questioningly, but he merely shook his head. "No questions yet. I'll have my office send you a reminder about our next appointment." He stood. "I'll show myself out."

Mary Nell finally succeeded in removing the lid of the box. Inside she saw a thick stack of paper, yellowed on the edges. The top sheet had one line, typed on an old manual typewriter, centered on the page. "The Life and Times of Bess Campbell."

Her eyes widened. "It's a book. Or a journal maybe. What am I supposed to do with this?"

Billy J. Yeats smiled at her, as he opened the door to leave. "Read it." He pulled the door closed behind him.

"Read it. What kind of game's that old woman playing with me?" Mary Nell set the box of paper down in disgust, stood up and walked around, went to the kitchen for a cup of coffee, paced, and finally sat back down and removed the manuscript from its box. "The Life and Times of Bess Campbell" was typed on a manual typewriter. The top left half of the cross on the capital "T" was missing so that it looked like a backward 7. The lower circle of lower case "a" was filled in making it into a pregnant worm. She turned the page and began to read.

> I was born ten years into the new century in Humansville, Missouri. I always thought that was a fine place for a human to be born. Not like Dog Town, Deer Run or Eagle's Nest. My parents, Angus James and Margaret Emma McDonald Campbell had been married for seven years before I was born. Papa asked Mamma what she wanted to name me. She said "Blessed One" but he thought she said "Bess Anne." The first accident of my life.

Mary Nell flipped several pages.

> Mamma's last child was finally another girl, Charlotte Jane. Mamma died shortly after Lottie's birth, and I never forgave her. Never forgave either of them for that matter. I was thirteen at the time, and Papa pulled me out of school to take care of little Lottie and the boys.

"Good grief. Page twenty-five and my grandma was just born. This is going to be slow going." Suddenly, Mary Nell had another idea. She flipped to the last page of the manuscript and read its single line.

> And so it falls to Lottie's daughter's daughter to set things right.

~~~

The seed catalog addressed to Buck Toomey was mis-delivered to the Floyd house. Walter looked at it incuriously and stuck it in his pocket. He'd drop it off at the tenant house as he went by. He poked his head into the den to tell Mary Nell that he was leaving. Her attention was on a stack of papers on her lap. He doubted that she even heard him speak.

Buck was walking across the road carrying a shovel and hoe when Walter drove by. Lulu was across the road chasing something – a ball, a squirrel or a low-flying bird. Walter slowed to Buck's pace, rolled down the window, handed out the catalog, and said, "This came to my place. You makin' a garden over there?"

Buck nodded. "That okay?"

Walter nodded. "Looks like you've been working hard at it. Looks good."

"Thanks. Just thought I'd plant a few greens for winter. They're easy to start from seed."

"Grow a lotta greens in that big plot."

"Yessir, guess I can. Thanks for the special delivery." Buck jumped across the ditch and walked into the line of trees that bordered the field. Lulu bounded back to him holding something in her mouth and dropping it at his feet. He picked it up and tossed it off to his right. Lulu made a long sweeping curve as she ran to the right, then zeroed in on the ball's position.

"A natural outrun," Walter said softly. "Mary Nell should see that."

~~~

The Fisher-Price CD player was at top volume playing "The Farmer in the Dell" as Bitsy danced on and around the furniture in her bedroom. On "Hi-Ho the Derry-O" she leaped onto the bed, landed on her butt, and bounced back to her feet. Then with the final "Farmer in the Dell" she bowed deeply, brushing her fingertips against the old quilt she loved.

From outside the room, Betty watched Bitsy in the mirror. She loved to see the drama imbued in all Bitsy's activities. Where did that come from, she wondered. Certainly not from herself or Dub. Both of them were about as dramatic as a drying sheet.

When she was in college, Betty came down firmly on the Nurture side of the Nature v. Nurture argument. But after Bitsy, she had changed camps. She knew she had never actively encouraged Bitsy to emote constantly. Bitsy just did so. From the moment she was born. Betty knew there weren't any actors in her family, but she wasn't sure about Dub's. She'd have to ask Mary Nell.

# Chapter 9

Mid-November was a strange time to plant a garden. But Buck was convinced that it wasn't too late to put out salad greens like lettuces, spinach, parsley, or onions and garlic. All he needed was a cover he could pull over the plants when it got below freezing. Of course, the standard method was a low tunnel built of curved PVC pipe, covered with plastic. But he thought that his solution of cut brush between the rows draped with plastic would work. It would keep the plastic off the plants, allow insulating air around them, and also disguise his plantings so he could surprise the Floyds with fresh greens in a couple weeks. Unless the mercury took too deep a dive too fast.

He whistled to Lulu. He wanted to look over his sprouting garden and see if he could rig a roller for the plastic he'd have to put on and take off, depending on sunshine and temperature. He had an idea of using a tall skinny tree denuded of branches and a piece of scavenged sewer pipe that he carried with him.

Lulu arrived, ball in mouth, and together they set off to the garden. About halfway there, Lulu began making those funny "mmwooof" noises caused by barking with a ball in her mouth. Buck thought there must be a skunk or fox in the area, but as they got closer to his garden plot, he saw a pair of khaki pants sticking up among the brush rows.

"Helloooo!" Buck called as he continued up the path. The person in pants straightened up and turned around, revealing himself to be in uniform. "What can I do for you, Deputy?" Buck laid down the pipe and approached the visitor with outstretched hand.

"Buck Toomey? This your garden?" The officer pointed to his badge, "I'm the sheriff not the deputy. Jones is the name."

"Sorry, Sheriff. Yep, this is my garden." Buck pointed at the ground beside him and Lulu lay down immediately but kept her eye on the visitor. "Help you with somethin'?"

The sheriff picked a leaf of newly sprouted oak-leaf lettuce, rubbed it between his fingers, smelled it, and tasted it. He spat it out and looked questioningly at Buck. "What is that?"

Buck grinned, "Lettuce. Baby lettuce."

"Hmm. That all you're growing?"

"Nope. Got mustard, spinach, turnips, onions an' garlic. Hope it stays warm long enough for 'em to get established."

A low growl from Lulu alerted them. The sheriff noticed some branches moving at the edge of the fenced field up the hill. "What's up there?"

Buck laughed, "Wouldn't go up there if I were you." He kept chuckling. "Sorry, but that reminds me of a joke I heard yesterday:

"See, this DEA officer stops in at a farm and talks with the ol' farmer there. He says, 'I need to inspect your farm for illegal drugs.'

"The ol' farmer looks him over and says, 'OK, but don't go in that field over there,' and points off to his right.

"The DEA guy gets huffy and says, 'Listen here, I am an officer of the Federal Government.' He pulls his badge out of his pocket. 'See this badge? It says I can look anywhere I want. Do you understand that?'

"The ol' farmer nods politely and says, 'I still wouldn't go in that field.'

"Now the officer was really pissed. He yells, 'See this badge? This badge means I can go in that field or any field. Do you understand?'

"The ol' farmer just nods and walks off.

"A little while later, the farmer hears screams and sees that officer running like the devil with a big bull chasing after him. The bull is gaining on him and his screams are getting louder.

"So the ol' farmer runs over to the fence and yells to the officer, 'Your badge! Show him your frickin' badge!'"

The sheriff paused, then snorted, "You telling me there's a bull up there in that pasture."

Buck continued to chuckle. "Yep. Walter Floyd moved Toro over there."

"Hmmp. OK. Good luck with your garden." The sheriff walked slowly back to his car parked just out of sight around the curve.

"Wonder what that was about, Lulu. Don't think he was lookin' for a salad."

~~~

*"Did you hear about that Dream Dinner Drawing Betty's doin'?"*

*"To my way of thinkin', a dream dinner's one I don't have to cook!"*

Rusty was putting up fliers all over town announcing Betty's "Dream Dinner" contest. For a twenty-dollar donation to feed the homeless, the winner got to choose the menu for a seven-course dinner for two. God, that would be a great treat for Shawna. But two things held him back from entering: the twenty-dollar entry fee and being Betty's brother. He could get around the first by using money he'd planned for something else. But he couldn't get around being Betty's brother. Betty wouldn't pick him. Couldn't. It wouldn't be fair. But it wasn't fair to him. He didn't ask to be her brother. Damn. It would have been such a cool Christmas present.

What would he want to eat if he could enter? He didn't know anything about fancy food. He liked most of the stuff Betty fixed but didn't know what any of it was called. He could just see his entry: "Tall green spiky things with oil and funny little seeds on top, followed by chopped up chunks of chicken with green sour things, red bits, mushrooms, onions and noodles." Yeah, that'd win for sure.

He tacked up the last flier on a telephone pole and saw his dad getting into a car with a tall gray-haired guy. Was that Charlie Keller? He walked into the café to pick up the ten-cents-each he'd earned distributing 200 fliers. "Hey, Betty. When did Dad and Charlie Keller become friends?" He took the twenty-dollar bill she handed him. He looked at it with dawning comprehension. Damn! His entry fee! Maybe he could get Shawna to put the entry in her name…. He shook himself to listen to Betty's reply to his question.

"…know each other."

"What? Say that again."

Betty slowly repeated with evident irritation, "I didn't know they were friends, but they do know each other. Why?"

Rusty shrugged, "I saw Dad getting into a car with Mr. Keller just now, and I think it's the same car that brought him home the other day. What's he up to?"

"I don't know. But getting out of the house is good for him, whatever the reason."

"Yeah, guess so. Thanks for the job." He waved the twenty at her as he left the café then got on his bike. Charlie Keller and his dad. What were they up to? Hmm, wonder if Shawna would enter the contest for them. It would be so great if they won. Course, it could be twenty dollars lost. But no, not lost. Given to the homeless for Thanksgiving dinner. But what a cool date that would be. Just the two of them in the entire café with their special dinner.

He dropped the front tire of his bike off the edge of the curb and had to grab a pickup's tailgate to keep from crashing. Jeez. It was dangerous to think and drive.

~~~

Surrounded by papers old and new, Mary Nell sat at the dining room table. It was the only space large enough to contain the numerous stacks she had created. She had gone through about fifty pages of Bess's manuscript, taking copious notes as she went. Since she didn't know what she might be expected to do about the information, she thought she needed to note everything. She had lists of all the minutia she'd so far discovered: names and dates of birth of the six boys who were bookended by Bess and Lottie – Matthew, Mark, Luke, John, Paul, and Silas; she knew the daily menus of the family and the number of loads of coal delivered each winter. Bess was nothing if not thorough. Dull but thorough.

Occasionally Bess told an amusing anecdote about the activities of the children or odd behavior of her father – like removing his false teeth and putting them into his pocket before eating. But most of Bess's writing was along the lines of the passage she had just read:

Papa arrived home each night at 6:30 during these years. He wanted his dinner to be served within fifteen minutes of his arrival. Several cooks had been dismissed because they couldn't comply with his wishes.

The boys needed to be washed and seated at the table when Papa entered the room. He allowed no talking until he had said the blessing, invariably "Bless, Oh God, this food we are about to partake and us the recipients of your bounty." After the Amen chorus decorous conversation was permitted.

Papa kept track of the cost of the food used in the preparation of each meal and would admonish anyone who failed to eat sufficient quantities with how much money he was wasting.

"Papa was a nutcase," Mary Nell mumbled as she made notes on a blue sheet of paper. She'd recently decided to color-code her notes to make them easier to organize.

"And you must have inherited that gene," said Walter from in the doorway. "Good God, Mary Nell! You're not studying for a Ph.D. on the life of Bess Campbell. Just read the damned manuscript and then ask that lawyer what you need to do. You are obsessed with this mess," he swept his arm above the top of the table.

"I know. I can't seem to stop. I'm concentrating on the details to keep from finding out what I'm expected to do. I'm kind of afraid to know."

"You? Afraid? Those words don't go together. Just do it, as that shoe ad says." He bent to kiss the top of her head.

"You're right." She picked up the manuscript and a notebook and leaned back in her chair to read. "Don't watch me. Go entertain yourself somewhere else." Walter nodded and left.

Mary Nell grabbed up several different colored papers and laid them around her. "Let's see, blue is for Papa."

Mary Nell slogged through several more pages of household details, lists of articles her brothers had written for the newspaper, and announcements of marriages, births, and deaths within the family. There was one section about unemployment and soup lines, but those were seen from a distance. Papa was never without work.

Finally, among the political slogans for the Roosevelt-Landon presidential race were four interesting paragraphs that Mary Nell copied onto pink paper, for Lottie:

> By 1936, Matthew and Mark had finished school and were working at the newspaper with Papa. Luke was reading the law and John was going into banking. The other two boys and Lottie were at the public school. Times were still hard. Everyone lived at home where I ran the household.
>
> Lottie was in the eighth grade. I had been in the eighth grade when Mamma died. I wanted Lottie to finish high school because I did not. Could not. But Lottie had no interest in school except as a central location for social encounters.
>
> She did well enough in school, however, until that fateful day when she met that frightful young man at the Alf Landon campaign rally in downtown Kansas City. After that, her only interest was him: talking to him, talking about him, dreaming of him, writing letters to him. If she had paid half as much attention to her schoolwork, she could have graduated with honors.
>
> Instead, her grades slipped precipitously. Papa was furious. He told her that he had no interest in supporting her daydreaming habits and that she must get her grades back up or leave school. She left home.

# Chapter 10

Betty had received twenty entries for her Dream Dinner contest. Many of her friends and family entered, and she figured it would lead to hard feelings if she chose the winner and did or did not pick someone she knew. So she decided to do a random drawing and get the head of the Homeless Shelter to draw the winning entry. After all he would get the proceeds to help pay for a big Thanksgiving Dinner at the shelter.

She flipped through the entries to see what had come in. She was amused to see that Walter really did write "Cheeseburger" on every line. Most of the other entries had shrimp cocktails, Caesar salad, filet mignon or salmon filet, baked potato, cheesecake or "Death by Chocolate" cake. Nice but not very interesting.

Two were interesting though. Buck's entry said simply, "I'll tell you if I win". But the best was Shawna Taylor's. She had described the dish rather than name it, as if she was afraid she'd get it wrong. Her first course was "creamy soup of winter squash and apple, seasoned with thyme." "Crisp baby lettuce and fresh herbs with a light lemon garlic vinaigrette" came next. Betty's favorite was the entrée – "tender slices of pork tenderloin braised in an apricot reduction with garlic mashed potatoes and julienned seasonal vegetables." She thought she's steal that for her menu.

She was surprised that Mary Nell hadn't entered. She was a good cook and an adventurous eater. Preparing her menu would have been a challenge but worth the effort. But Mary Nell was holed up reading some old manuscript and not paying attention to much else. She hadn't even picked up Bitsy for several days. And that was unusual. She always said she had withdrawal if she missed more than a day or two.

Maybe she'd just drop in on Mary Nell this afternoon when things were slow and her part-timer was there. She'd take Bitsy with her. That ought to get Mary Nell's head out of bunch of old papers.

~~~

Bitsy ran into the café trailing scarf and sweater. "Oh, Mommy! We had the best time today! We got to go watch the High School Kids build a Float! It was so cool! They took Kleenex and stuffed it in Holes and made a Big Chicken. And they're going to put it in a Parade!"

"Wow, Bits. That sounds like fun. We'll go watch the parade next Saturday afternoon, OK?" Bitsy's head nodded like a bobble-headed doll. "Want a snack now? Then I thought we'd go see Grandmary and Gramps." She set a glass of milk and a sliced apple in front of her highly-wound daughter.

"Oh yes, Mommy! I could tell them all about the Float!" Bitsy glowed in anticipation.

Betty shook her head in wonder. She should have named this kid Meryl Streep. "OK, kiddo. Eat up, then we'll go." She checked with her part-timer, cleared Bitsy's dishes, and they headed to the car. Bitsy did a couple of Peter Pan jumps on the way.

When they arrived at Mary Nell and Walter's it looked like nobody was home. The curtains were drawn and the big oak front door was closed. Bitsy took no notice, but rang the bell happily, leaping from one foot to the other. Finally, the door opened to a bedraggled Mary Nell.

"Are you sick, Grandmary? We can get you some soup." Bitsy's exuberance turned to worried concern in an instant.

"No, Sweetpea, I'm not sick. I've just been busy." She glanced down at herself, then sheepishly up at Betty. "Or obsessed, according to Walter. But come in. Come in." She bent to hug a happily smiling Bitsy. "Oooh, I missed you. I'm so glad you came to see me." She led them inside and offered them hot chocolate or tea.

Bitsy looked hopefully at her mother, "I think I could have a leeetle hot chocolate. Right, Mommy?"

Betty nodded, and Bitsy leaped into the air. "Yes!" she cried. She spotted Roberta curled up in a big chair. "I'll pet on Roberta while the chocolate gets hot. OK?"

Mary Nell nodded and went with Betty to the kitchen and put the milk on to heat. "I'm glad you came by. I've gotten immersed in Aunt Bess's story. After pages and pages of minute details about everything under the sun, she's teased me with a mystery. Here, let me show you." She walked Betty into the dining room and showed her the stacks of pages she had been making and summarized what she knew of the family.

"Look at this. I just got to it a little while ago. I haven't even had time to enter it into my notes." She handed a few pages of the manuscript to Betty and pointed at a paragraph near the top. "Start there."

> Just before Pearl Harbor threw us into war, I got a letter from Lottie. The first I had had in over four years. It was dated November, 1941, and mailed from Detroit, Michigan.
>
> With the others enlisted or married, only Mark and I still lived at home with an aging and perennially cranky Papa. So it was with Mark that I shared the

news from Lottie. She was married to a trumpet player and singing with his band. Their home was St. Louis, but they were currently touring, and planning to be in Kansas City just after the New Year. She wanted to see me and any of the brothers who where available. She enclosed a review of the band from the *Detroit Free Press* and the particulars for their Kansas City appearance. I hoped Mark would go with me, but whether he did or not, I was going to see my sister,

When the time came to see Lottie, I had a problem. Mark enlisted in the Army the day after Pearl Harbor, so I was without an escort to the Muehlebach Ballroom where Lottie's band was playing. I would not ask Papa to go. I was unwilling to put myself or Lottie through that ordeal. So I asked both Matthew and Luke to accompany me. I was sure their wives would not object since they were going with me and were unlikely to drink too much in my company.

We arrived at the ballroom early. I had not anticipated having to pay a cover charge to get in, but I insisted on paying the entire amount. It had been my idea. We were given a table not far from the stage and each ordered a cocktail. I was thirsty and drank mine too quickly. I was not used to spirits, and the incipient dizziness did nothing to allay my nervousness.

Soon enough, the band came onstage and began to play a snappy dance tune. I craned to see the trumpet players, trying to pick out the one married to Lottie. After two numbers, the leader announced their star singer was up next. Rousing applause brought out a steamy brunette in a low-cut, tight-fitting dress. The leader bowed to her and announced her name: Lola Bell. I was stunned, unable to believe this sultry creature was my baby sister. And then she started to sing. Everything else disappeared.

Later, Lottie/Lola introduced us to her husband, Tony. He was the handsome one I had decided upon. But his manner was less than polite to us. He nodded curtly at each of us, then smacked Lottie on her posterior and told her to hurry up, the next set was about to begin. She begged us not to leave until she had more time to talk with us and went backstage to change for her next set.

When she came to the table next, she apologized for not being able to stay. Tony had made plans and she had to leave with him. She thanked us for coming, gave us each a hug, and slipped an envelope into my hand while muttering in my ear, "Shh. It's better this way." With that, she left.

When I got home, I found a torn slip of paper stuffed into the envelope. On it was written three lines: Julia Edith Campbell; Born Memphis, Tennessee; March 23, 1939.

"God, Mary Nell. Do you think your grandmother gave up a child when she was, what, sixteen?" Betty scanned the pages again, looking for more information.

"I don't know. I have to read the rest. But I need to make my notes first."

"Are you nuts? Why don't you read the whole thing, then come back and make notes. Then you'd know what was important."

"Then I'd be too biased by my expectations to see everything that's there. Or so I keep telling myself." Mary Nell took back the pages from Betty and carefully stacked them on top of the others. "Oh, damn. The hot chocolate! I nearly forgot."

She ran to the kitchen to save the milk, while Betty looked around in wonder. She thought she knew Mary Nell, but she never suspected she'd get like this. Walter was right. She was obsessed.

Mary Nell and Bitsy came in with mugs of hot chocolate and a plate of cookies. "Mommy, one cookie wouldn't hurt, would it? You could have one, too."

"OK, Bits. One. And Mary Nell, I think you should put a splash of somethin' strong in your cocoa. You need to chill." Betty looked at Mary Nell with concern. She looked old and worn.

"Then I'll get you some *ice*, Grandmary. That will make you chilly." For the first time, Mary Nell's smile reached her eyes.

~~~

Walter had felt silly carrying in a cowplop and some chewed up weeds to the county extension agent, but he wanted to know what was wrong with Toro. A week later, the agent called him with the results. She read to him from the report that identified the plant material as a wild hibiscus called a "marsh mallow." The cow feces contained traces of the hibiscus, but an even larger amount of lettuce leaves. Had he been feeding lettuce?

He assured the agent that he had not been feeding lettuce, thanked her, and hung up more confused than ever. Where the hell did that bull get lettuce? And those spiky-leaved plants weren't hemp at all. He couldn't wait to tell Buck. He chuckled to himself. He'd tell the sheriff he bet those *marsh mallows* were left over from that campfire.

~~~

Shawna's mother helped her put her hair into a French braid. Shawna wanted to dress up a little for the Homecoming dance. "I thought you were supposed to dance in what you wore to the game," Diane Taylor lisped through the hairpins in her mouth.

"Yeah, we were. But that didn't take into account the cold rain all afternoon. Oh, Mom, it was awful. The floats all melted, and the little kids that came to see them in the parade were so disappointed. The game was a mud wrestling match. By the time it was over, everybody in the stands was almost as miserable as the guys on the field. At least we won."

She and Rusty were going to dinner then to the dance, but she insisted they put on dry clothes first. And let her do something with her wet, straggling hair.

"Isn't it late in the year for Homecoming?" Diane was having trouble with one strand of hair that wanted to turn left rather than right.

"Yeah. It was a scheduling problem. One of the high schools had to be last, and we got lucky. But they moved Fall Festival up, so it all worked out." Shawna slumped in the chair. "Aren't you about done?"

"Mmm-hmm. When's Rusty picking you up?" Diane twisted a rubber band around the ends of the braid. "You're so lucky to have such thick, beautiful hair." She smoothed the sides again and spritzed it with hairspray.

"Thanks, Mom. Rusty'll be here in about ten minutes. I've got to get dressed." She hurried from the room, leaving her mother looking wistfully after her. Shawna was a good kid. But so young with so much to learn.

A few minutes later the doorbell rang. Pete dashed to answer it, beating Maisie, Diane and Shawna. He threw open the heavy door, saw that it was Rusty, and turned to walk away. "Peter! You are being very rude. You invite Rusty in." Diane tried to impress good manners on her son with little success.

"Come on in," Pete mumbled. "Whew! You smell like flowers."

"Peter!" His mother's look wilted Pete's cockiness. He quickly backed away from the door.

Rusty shook off his coat and wiped his feet before entering. "Hi, Mrs. Taylor. Maisie." Turning to Shawna, his face blazed as he once again beheld an angel. "Gee, you look wonderful. How'd you get so beautiful so fast?"

Shawna smiled at him and told him he looked good, too. "Are you ready to go? We won't be late, Mom." She got her coat from the closet. Rusty took it and held it for her. Somehow, he had one sleeve twisted to the front so that she couldn't get her arm in it. After several attempts, she took the coat from him and put it on alone.

"Sorry." His face blazed again. He opened the door for her, caught his toe on the throw-rug, and stumbled into the closet door.

Shawna grinned at her mother and whispered, "Isn't he cute?"

Her mother nodded, smiling. He was cute. She remembered how it felt to have a boy stumbling all over himself for her. She hoped Shawna would be careful. Falling in love could be very dangerous.

# Chapter 11

"Fold Tab A into Slot B, my ass!" Betty slammed down the piece of black felt she was trying to fashion into a Pilgrim bonnet.

Bitsy leaped to her side and placed her palm on her mother's cheek. "Don't say *ass*, Mamma. It makes you mad when you say *ass*."

Betty looked over the top of her glasses at her daughter. "You're right, Bits. I shouldn't say *ass*." She patted Bitsy's hand, then mumbled under her breath, "I shouldn't have to try to follow these damned directions either."

"Mamma," Bitsy picked up two of the larger pieces of felt and put them on her head. "Will this be a hat?"

"That's a good question. It's supposed to be a bonnet. But I haven't gotten there yet." She looked again at the instructions, and shook her head. "When is your Pilgrim play?"

"I think it's tomorrow, but it might be next week." Bitsy, unconcerned with logistics, looked at herself in the mirror over the hall table. "How will it stay on?"

Betty snorted, "It won't if I can't figure out how to get the darned thing to fit together. Here, give it back to me and go listen to music or something. Mamma needs to concentrate."

Bitsy took the half-formed bonnet off her head, then squinched closed her brown eye and studied the hat with her blue one. "Yeah. It needs work. But you can do it, Mamma, if you put your mind to it." She scampered off down the hall to play in her room.

Betty looked after her with amusement. It really sucked to hear her own words of encouragement come back at her. She needed to watch what she said.

She held three pieces together, looking back and forth from the directions to the pieces in her hands, and suddenly stiffened. "Oh! That's how they fit." As she reached for the bottle of Elmer's Glue to solidify her epiphany, the phone rang. "Get the phone, please, Bitsy," she yelled down the hallway. She quickly glued and held the stubborn fabric together, keeping a grip on it as she went to get the phone.

She heard Bitsy answer the phone politely then yell, "Mamma, some man wants you to dream about dinner."

Betty smiled. "Thanks, Bits. I've got it." She picked up the phone and spoke to Reverend Black from the Open Arms Homeless Shelter. After she arranged to meet him at the café later that afternoon, she discovered her fingers had stuck to the bonnet string she had just attached.

~~~

Walter had insisted last night that Mary Nell leave her manuscript for the evening and have dinner and see a movie with him. He had been right, she realized, both that she was obsessed and that she needed a break. When she couldn't keep track of the plot of the silly chick-flick he'd chosen to please her, she knew she was overly tired. After the movie, she meditated for over an hour and nearly returned to the feeling of calm she had found on that afternoon she spent in the pine grove. Too bad it was too cold to return there. She would have loved to sit in that resting place.

This morning she made herself eat a bowl of cereal and drink her first cup of coffee before going into the dining room to read more of Aunt Bess's "Life and Times." Her first task was to start a new data sheet for Julia Edith Campbell, on yellow paper she thought.

Bess loved lists. Lists of places the boys fought, the food and gasoline ration points they used and saved, the names of wounded or killed relatives, friends and neighbors, war bonds purchased. Mary Nell conscientiously noted the information Bess recorded, all the while looking for more information about her grandmother.

She read through many pages of the manuscript and noted that Matthew, Mark, John and Paul were killed in various locations in the Pacific. Luke was severely wounded and eventually lost a leg to infection. Silas's wounds healed while he was hospitalized in California, and when he was released, he married one of the nurses and settled there.

Finally, toward the end of the war years, Mary Nell found Lottie mentioned:

> After Luke came home missing a leg, Papa just gave up. His boys were dead, wounded, or gone. His younger daughter was as good as dead, and his elder was fast becoming an eccentric old maid. His funeral was May 5, 1945. He didn't live to see the war end.
>
> In September, 1945, I abandoned my paltry research efforts and hired a detective in Memphis, Tennessee. He was a returning veteran who had been a policeman before the war. He seemed worth taking a chance on, so I sent him the information Lottie had given me and the few other bits I had been able to gather. I also asked

him to find Lottie or Lola Bell or whoever she had become. I wanted more than six words and a date.

After this brief mention, Bess returned to lists: dealing with Papa's estate and legal fees, people who attended the funeral, floral tributes received. A few sad paragraphs about learning to live alone in the large house were followed by more lists of food purchased and meals prepared. Then "Lottie" jumped out of the text again.

> Ten years after I'd last seen Lottie, my Memphis detective located her. She was living in De Soto, Missouri, with a daughter. Her "husband" had been killed in France, leaving her to do piecework in a factory that made women's clothing. If he had married her, she would have had widow's benefits. As it was, she had what she could earn working in the only factory she could find that would employ women after the men came home. I didn't find out, then or ever, why she had stopped singing.

> I wrote to her. I told her Papa had died, what became of the boys, and asked her to come home. She could live here and not have to work. Her daughter could go to the same school we had attended. I enclosed train fare. And I waited for her reply.

> It took her nearly four months to use the train tickets. I had no word from her until a worn woman and skinny girl appeared at my door in the spring of 1952.

> Lottie's daughter, Janet was almost ten when they came to live with me. She was a quiet, sickly child with none of the high spirits of her mother. She was happiest when curled around a cat in the wing chair in the parlor with her head hidden behind a book. She did well enough in school considering the time she lost to illness. She caught every cold, sneezed at every dust mote, and broke out in hives with every bite of unusual food.

> Lottie dragged around the house initially, taking little interest in anything but caring for her child. I

suggested that she sing in the choir at church, but she would neither sing nor discuss it. Eventually she found a job at a dress shop near the house. She said she could not stand it anymore, being shut up in the darkness of the old house. Besides, she did not like to ask me for spending money, and I did keep a tight hold on the purse strings, partly, I now think, to control Lottie's movements. I thought she could not leave if she could not afford to.

"Oh, Aunt Bess! I can tell you that won't work." Mary Nell leaned back, rubbed her eyes, and remembered how she'd tried to stop Dub from leaving. Nothing she did, active or passive, made any difference. When people want to leave, they leave.

She read on, finding lists of Janet's absences from school, doctors consulted, and medicines prescribed and taken before she found another surprising section:

Lottie never inquired about what I had done or what I found out about the name on the envelope she had given me all those years ago. Since I had no information to share, I did not bring up the name either.

Then in 1955, my ongoing employment of the Memphis detective paid off. He located Julia Edith Campbell, now Edie Smith, and her baby daughter living in Southaven, Mississippi, just outside Memphis.

I was unsure about what to do. I did not know how Lottie would react nor what effect this information would have on Janet, who at twelve was bumping into puberty with all its emotional turmoil. I worried about what finding a never-known sister would do to her.

After several sleepless nights, I finally sat Lottie down and told her the news. I was stunned at her reaction. She merely nodded and left the room. I decided to wait for her to bring up the subject again. She did not.

~~~

The Ladies arrived at the café together that afternoon. Betty was ready for them, took their orders, served them, and retired to another table to work on a press release for the results of her Dream Dinner drawing. She would have it all written but the winner's name and menu and get it to the newspaper office before the editor left. That way it would make tomorrow's edition of the town's only weekly.

She paid little attention to the conversations around her until raucous laughter caused her to look to The Ladies Corner.

*"He did what?"*

*"He slid on his knees across the floor and crashed into the refreshment table."*

*"Lord, was he hurt?"*

*"Have you seen him?"*

*"I did. He was sneaking around to keep from being seen, but I saw enough. What a shiner!"*

*"How'd he get a shiner?"*

*"Oh, that was from Steve Wilson's fist."*

*"Steve Wilson hit him?"*

*"Yeah, but I don't think he meant to. He was trying to keep the punch bowl from flipping over and missed his grab."*

*"And popped him in the eye?"*

*"It was that or Rusty'd have been really 'punched'!"*

*"What started the whole thing?"*

*"Rusty and Shawna were dancing, and Rusty started getting fancy. He twirled Shawna, somehow caught his foot on hers, fell to his knees and slid across the floor."*

*"He is such a klutz!"*

*"Yeah. And being near Shawna makes him worse."*

At that point, Betty could stand it no longer. She marched up to The Ladies Corner and demanded, "Are you talking about Rusty?" The Ladies nodded meekly. "I didn't hear everything. You said he has a shiner?"

Charlie Keller turned around to Betty. "They sure did. He fell at the Homecoming dance. Been hiding out since then. Didn't want anyone to know."

The Ladies glared at Charlie. It was their news! Bonnie finally spoke up, "That's right. I hear he even skipped school, he's been so embarrassed."

Betty nodded and walked away. Charlie turned back to his newspaper, and The Ladies left shortly afterwards. Betty watched them leave thinking they were probably right. She could imagine that very thing happening to Rusty. And she hadn't seen him in several days. Poor kid. He must be mortified. She'd do him a favor and leave him alone.

~~~

Two hours later, Reverend Black and most of the Dream Dinner Contest entrants had gathered in the café. Betty gave a short speech thanking everyone for entering the contest and saying how excited she was to prepare some lucky person his, or her, Dream Dinner. Reverend Black said how happy he was that Betty had raised over $400.00 for the shelter and that they would be able to pay for both Thanksgiving and Christmas dinner with the money raised.

Betty held a hat above Reverend Black's eye level, and he pulled out the winning entry. He handed it to Betty to read. She burst into laughter, "Walter Floyd!" That would be an easy dinner to prepare: seven cheeseburgers. She was about to announce that very thing, when Walter caught her eye.

"Thanks, Betty. Before you say anything I have a couple of questions about the rules of the contest. First, do I have to be the one to eat the meal?"

She frowned, thought a second, and said, "No. The rules didn't say that."

"OK, then. Does it have to be the menu I entered? Or could you cook something else?"

Betty puzzled again for a second, "I guess I could cook whatever you want. Why? You want something besides seven cheese-burgers?"

Everyone laughed, and Walter nodded. "OK. I assign my Dream Meal to Shawna Taylor and ask you to cook her menu entry. Seems like she deserves something for going out with Rusty."

The diner erupted with laughter. Walter looked pleased. Shawna blushed and looked even more pleased. Rusty wasn't there to hear the ribbing. But he'd hear about it soon enough, Betty thought.

After everyone congratulated Walter and Shawna, the café cleared of nearly everyone. Buck lingered a moment to say quietly to Betty, "Good thing I didn't win." He winked and walked out the door.

She watched his cocky stride down the sidewalk. What was with that cowboy, anyway?

# Chapter 12

He slammed another cabinet door. What was going on? Rusty couldn't find anything in the house to eat that didn't require cooking. Well except some fruit and a box of high fiber cereal. And milk. What happened to all the snack foods his dad always kept around the house? He was starving and a banana and a bowl of All-Bran wasn't going to cut it.

Damn, he guessed he'd have to go into town. He eye had faded to a pale greenish-yellow. Maybe nobody would notice it if he kept his hat pulled down. Yeah, fat chance!

He'd been holed up in his room feigning deathly illness since Sunday morning when he woke up with a seriously bruised face. How could he be so clumsy? He had been having such a good time, showing off his moves to Shawna, and the next thing he knew, his face slammed into Steve Wilson. Steve Wilson! The geekiest kid in the class. He'd never live it down.

Rusty stayed in his bedroom except when he was sure his dad was asleep. Then he'd sneak food. Enough to last for several hours. And tell his dad he didn't feel like eating. But now there was nothing to eat. Nothing! How could there be nothing? There was plenty left when he made his last raid. His dad couldn't have eaten it all.

He put on a hoodie and a baseball cap. He pulled the brim low over his eyes, quietly left the house, and jumped on his bike. He had to raise the brim to see. God, he didn't need to wreck the bike now.

When he arrived at the Food King he pulled his hat back down, kept his head lowered, and headed to the chips aisle. He picked up potato chips, corn chips, and bean dip. He grabbed a package of chocolate cookies and a two-liter bottle of Coke on the way to the checkout. Damn! There was Helen Poole in line. What Helen knew, The Ladies knew; and what The Ladies knew, everybody knew.

His dad was gone again when he got home. Rusty hadn't checked before he left, assuming his dad was asleep, but now the curtains were open and a dirty bowl was in the sink. His dad probably ate the All-Bran and banana.

He wandered through the house, thinking hard. The only idea he came up with was to call Betty. He'd avoided her since the Homecoming Catastrophe, but he guessed he'd better call her. She usually had good ideas.

~~~

Pete Taylor was excited. He was going out on an adventure with Walter Floyd. He liked Walter. Walter didn't treat him like a kid. He talked to him like a man. Nobody else did that. His mother babied him and his sisters treated him like a pest. Well, he was a pest sometimes. But Walter was different, and Pete was different with Walter.

Walter had only told Pete that he needed help solving a mystery. Pete had asked if he needed to bring any special equipment, but Walter said no, he had everything they'd need. Pete was so antsy he could barely eat breakfast before Walter picked him up. Then he was full of questions: where were they going? What were they looking for? What was the mystery?

Buck's observations, the sheriff's visit, the results of the tests at the county extension—Walter slowly told Pete the story of Toro. Pete interrupted constantly asking questions. Walter patiently made it through all the known facts. "So that's why I want your help. I want us to look over everything in that pasture where Toro was and see if we can find out what's been going on."

"How will we know what to look for?" Pete was bouncing up and down in the seat of the pickup, eager to get started. Walter parked the truck beside the gate into the pasture and handed a long stick to Pete. "Here, carry this. We might need it." He thought Pete might feel more comfortable holding a possible weapon while walking through the tall grass.

They went into the pasture after Walter unchained the gate. It had been a while since Toro had been there to eat any of the grass. It came up to his knees and Pete's waist. It was not going to be easy to find anything in this jungle.

"You start walking along the fence going that way, and I'll go this way. We'll meet at the far side; then we'll swing in a ways and go back, OK?" Walter started walking away from the road while Pete went parallel to it along the fence line. After only a few minutes Walter heard Pete yell. He went at a run, worried Pete had found a snake. But Pete grinned and pointed at a patch of light green plants. Lettuce? Walter bent over and picked a leaf. He smelled it, felt it, and finally tasted it. "Lettuce! I'll be damned! Good job, Pete."

Pete glowed. He was proud that he'd found the lettuce patch. It wasn't visible from the road because of some tall weeds growing in the fence line. But it wasn't far from the road, either.

Walter looked at the ground carefully. It didn't look like it had been tilled. But it was clear of weeds and grass. He turned in a circle, looking around to see if anything came to mind. Then he saw movement in the field across the road at the top of the hill.

Mitch Spears' land. He closed his brown eye and squinted through his blue one. Hmmp. He called Pete to his side and pointed, "What do you see up there?"

"A cow."

"I think it's a bull. I think Toro could see the Spears' bull from here. I think he scratched at the ground to show that other bull how big and tough he was. He scratched away all the grass."

Pete nodded, using the same short dip of the head that Walter did.

"Now, if we could figure out how the seed got there." Walter took off his cap, rubbed his head and scratched his nose.

Scratching his own nose while Walter put his cap back on, Pete watched Walter's every move. He looked down at the ground near the fence and saw a tattered piece of white paper stuck in the weeds. "Look at that," he said while scrambling into the edge of the weeds to retrieve it. He pulled it out of briars and handed it to Walter.

Turning it over, Walter saw a green drawing and a few letters faded and partially obscured by time and rain. "Seeded," he said pointing to the first word. "S-I-M-something-S-O-something. Can you make out that letter?"

Pete looked closely and said, "I think it's a P"

Walter sounded out "Simp-so. Simpson! Black-Seeded Simpson. It's a kind of lettuce. This is a seed packet. Way to go, Pete!" He clapped Pete on the shoulder.

Pete beamed. He'd found the lettuce and the seed packet. The mystery was solved. He was as good as a Hardy Boy!

Walter squinted at the seed packet. Now where the hell did that come from?

When Walter dropped Pete off at home, he praised his accomplishment to Pete's mother and sisters. He was glad that Pete had been the one to find the lettuce and seed packet. Pete seemed to grow several inches taller that morning.

~~~

At home, he found Mary Nell intently studying the manuscript, as he knew he would. He left her to it. She'd wear out or finish, one. He wasn't sure which.

Her face softened as she glanced at Walter, but turned serious again as she returned to noting the lists of Janet's illnesses, grades in school, clothing purchases and visits to friends on the green paper she'd chosen for Janet. Her mother was a dull child. She didn't do anything interesting, or at least nothing Aunt Bess mentioned. Of course, it was interesting to Mary Nell to learn anything of her mother's childhood. Grandma never said much, and she didn't remember her mother ever mentioning being a kid. Then she spotted a real surprise:

> Just before Janet's fourteenth birthday, a letter arrived from the same Memphis detective I had kept on retainer for the past twelve years. He wrote that Edie Smith was in trouble. She had lost her job and was about to be evicted from her home. Did I want him to do anything?
>
> I thought hard about what to do. Lottie had never discussed Edie with me. I knew I had to make the decision. Lottie would not. I wrote to the detective, enclosing a money order for $100.00 and a letter to Edie. Then, as I had done with Lottie, I waited.
>
> Two weeks later I got my first telephone call from the detective. He said he needed instructions immediately

and could not wait on the mails. And with that introduction he told me a strange tale.

He had, he assured me, delivered my letter and money order to Edie as soon as he had received them. She was very surprised to find that she had any family. Her adoptive parents had divorced, her father had died of alcohol poisoning, and her mother and she were estranged. She thanked him for delivering the money and information, and he left.

A few days later, his office received a message from Edie. She needed for him to do something for her, she said. Could he come to her house that evening? There was something she wanted him to deliver to me.

He agreed. He arrived at her house just before dark. He knocked on the door, but it was not latched and swung open at his touch. He looked inside and saw a playpen sitting in the middle of the room, with a screaming child occupying it. On the floor in front of the playpen was a piece of plain paper with large hand lettered instructions: "Please take her to Bess Campbell in Kansas City. It's the best way. Edie."

"My God! Another abandoned child. This sounds like made-up melodrama." Mary Nell was talking to herself and making notes when Walter came in. She briefed him on what she'd discovered, then asked, "So what have you been up to?" She shook herself, then laid down her papers and gave him her full attention.

Walter noticed her efforts and reached for her hand. He squeezed it and told her of his morning with Pete.

Mary Nell's eyes twinkled, "You should have asked me."

"I did ask you, but your head was so far into Bess Campbell's business you didn't hear me. What do you know about it anyway?"

She told him of finding the old seed packet in her jewelry bag a few weeks ago. She'd stuck it in her jeans pocket, planning to show it to him. Later that day, she was out for a walk and saw a patch of raw earth inside the pasture where Walter kept the bull. She had the mischievous idea of seeing if those old seeds would germinate. So she sprinkled the seeds on the soil, then walked on it to push the seed into the ground, and laid some fallen branches on top of the area to keep Toro away. She guessed she'd dropped the seed packet.

When she'd gone back later to check on it, she'd seen some of the seeds had sprouted, so she moved the branches away to give the plants light. She planned to keep quiet about it until the lettuce matured, then bring it home for a salad and surprise Walter. But the letter about Aunt Bess arrived, the lawyer brought the manuscript, and she forgot all about it.

"Well I'll be double damned! Here I've been traipsin' all over the county, carryin' cowplop in for analysis, and you planted the damned lettuce. Son of a bitch!"

"I'm sorry, Walter. I didn't know you were worrying about it. I only did it for a lark."

Walter stared at her, then exploded in deep belly laughs. He laughed until tears ran down his cheeks. His chest heaved and he held his stomach, moaning. Occasionally he interrupted himself with disconnected words: "hemp," "sheriff," "stoned." Wiping his eyes, he leaned over and kissed Mary Nell with a loud smack. "I love you. I haven't laughed like this in years." As he left the room, gurgles and shakes dropped in his wake.

Mary Nell shook her head. What the hell was that all about?

The doorbell rang just as Walter entered the hall. He straightened his face and opened the door to find a grinning Buck holding out a large bag filled with lettuce. Walter spewed out a loud "ha ha ha" and waved Buck inside. He couldn't manage words, only gasps and giggles, as he led Buck to the dining room.

Once there, he pointed to Mary Nell and sat down, grasping himself around the middle. Buck looked alarmed, but Mary Nell said, "Hey, Buck. Don't worry about Walter. He's gotten tickled and has to laugh 'til it's over. What's up?"

Buck held out the bag to Mary Nell. "Thought you might like some lettuce for supper."  When she hiccupped a giggle, he looked stricken. "Did I screw up? Don't you eat lettuce?"

"We eat lettuce. Sorry. We love lettuce. It's just a silly story Walter was telling before you got here." She wiped her eyes and made shushing motions at Walter who was still gasping. "This is nice. Did you grow it?"

"Yep. In that field up the hill from my house. I covered it with brush so it would be a surprise."

"Surprise! Hoo-hoo-ha!" Walter dissolved again.

"Huh-huh. Don't mind him. It's beautiful lettuce. Thank you!" She pulled a leaf from the bag and bit off a piece. "Sweet and tender." She chewed a moment, then said with a glint in her eye, "Have you shown this to Betty? I bet she'd like to buy some for her café."

# Chapter 13

*"Tommy McCann seems to be getting out more."*

*"Yep. I saw him with Charlie Keller the other day driving down Maple."*

*"I wonder what those two old farts are up to?"*

When Tommy McCann left the house, Rusty was ready for him. He jumped on his bike ready to follow the old Plymouth that his dad got into. Charlie Keller's, Rusty was sure. Careful to keep out of sight, Rusty stayed along the side of the road or on the sidewalk. He was astonished when the car turned into the parking lot of First Presbyterian Church.

He set his bike down next to a tree and walked around the edge of the lot until he could see the side door. His dad and Charlie Keller went inside, greeting others as they entered. As the door closed, Rusty saw a sign on it. He crept close enough to read it: OA Meets Here" was followed by a list of days and times.

"OA? What's OA?" he muttered. At least he knew where his dad had been going, if not why.

He retrieved his bike and rode it to the café. Betty was busy when he got there, so he sat at the counter and waited, trying to keep his head down and out of view.

"How's the eye?" Betty set a glass of tea in front of him. She tried to look at it, but his chin was tucked into his Adam's apple. She ducked down to counter height and looked up at him.

"Let it go, Betty. This is important."

"What? Something wrong? Dad okay?"

"Nothing's wrong, exactly. And Dad, who knows? Remember I told you about him disappearing, then cleaning all the snacks out of the house? Well, today I followed him to church."

"Church? You sure?"

"Yes, I'm sure. I told you I followed him. He went with Charlie Keller to the Presbyterian church. They went in a door that said OA met there. What's OA?"

Betty's eyes widened, "Ah, now I get it."

"Well I don't." Rusty's concern turned to irritation with Betty's know-it-all attitude.

"OA is Overeaters Anonymous. He's going to meetings to get control of his eating. It's like drunks go to Alcoholics Anonymous. You know, AA."

"Oh. Well, that's okay then." Rusty drew his eyebrows together as he though about it. "Does that mean he's a food junkie?"

"I don't know. I think we need to talk to him before we jump to any conclusions. But I also think he'll tell us when he's ready. Let's leave it be." She tapped her pencil on the edge of the counter. "I think this is a good thing. Don't worry so."

Rusty looked doubtful, but nodded. "OK. I'll wait for him to talk."

"Good plan. Oh, hey. Do you want to go see Bitsy in her Pilgrim play tonight? Her kindergarten class is putting on a Thanksgiving play tonight at 6:30."

"Yeah. And I'll see if Dad'll come."

"Bring Shawna, too."

"Yeah, maybe. If she's still talking to me." Rusty touched his eye and ducked his head.

"Oh, I'm sure she'd still talk to you if you called her. You haven't seen her since the dance?"

"Naw." He tucked his chin deeper into his shirt collar.

"Then you don't know." Betty's eyes twinkled with untold tales.

"Don't know what?"

"Walter won the Dream Dinner drawing and gave it to Shawna. Said it was a consolation prize for going out with you." She answered his skeptical glance with another nod. "Really! You need to call that girl, little bro."

Rusty raised his chin and let the corner of his mouth twitch. "See you tonight, sis."

As he climbed on his bike, Rusty glanced at the clock on the bank across the street. Yeah, school was out. He knew he couldn't hide out forever and guessed it was time to go see Shawna.

She was ambling up the street when he arrived. "Hey," he pulled up beside her and dropped a foot to steady the bike.

"Hey." She looked at his face closely, reached to touch his still yellow skin but pulled back at his involuntary flinch. "Still hurt?"

"Some. It's better. Sorry I haven't called." Eyes cast down, he looked like a six-year-old.

"You been sick?" She watched him carefully.

"Naw." A flush spread up his neck. "I was too embarrassed to come to school. Stupid, huh?"

"Kinda." She waited.

"Well, I'm over it. I'll be there tomorrow."

"Good," she still waited. He was getting his balance!

"So, anyway. Bitsy's Pilgrim Play's tonight at 6:30. I wondered if you'd wanna go."

"OK."

"OK. I'll pick you up at 6:15." He rode off down the street. When he was about a block away, Shawna was sure she heard him shout, "Hot Damn!"

~~~

Tommy McCann insisted on sitting in the back seat. "You'll want that pretty girl up next to you." He watched the red creep up Rusty's neck. That boy sure could blush. "I'll get a ride home afterwards so you can take her home."

"No thanks, Dad. Betty said for us all to go to the café for cocoa after."

"You're a good kid, Rusty. I don't tell you that enough." Tommy watched the red rise again. Shoot, Rusty could win a blushing contest.

After picking up Shawna, he arrived at the school to find Betty, Mary Nell and Walter had saved them seats near the front. This was Bitsy's big debut and the whole family turned out for it.

Stevi Johnson, Bitsy's teacher, opened by telling the audience to cast their minds back to the 1620's. The pilgrims had arrived at Plymouth with little in the way of supplies and less in the practical knowledge it would take to survive in the inhospitable climate and unknown surroundings. With that, several "Indians" in breechcloth-covered khaki slacks and feathered headgear appeared and stood around the edge of the stage, holding ears of corn or stuffed animal toys.

Three pilgrim men with obligatory black hats and beards entered the stage. Each carried a string of Mardi Gras beads or a piece of bright fabric. As the pilgrims moved from group to group of Indians, they would exchange a strand of beads for an ear of corn or the fabric for a stuffed toy. Stevi provided voice-over, describing the ways the settlers learned to trade with the natives.

The girls came on stage next, carrying pumpkins and loaves of bread. As Stevi described the successful harvest, a girl in a particularly well-put-together bonnet, Betty noticed, told the men that dinner was ready and to bring their friends. "We got lots!"

Someone shoved a picnic table into the middle of the stage, and pilgrims and Indians sat down together. One of the boys stood at the head of the table and said in a quavering voice, "Thank you God for all this food. Amen."

Rusty nudged Betty, "Where's Bitsy? I don't see her on stage?"

"Shhh. I don't know. I don't see her either."

As everyone ate a pumpkin cookie, Stevi talked about the food that was served at the dinner, bringing groans from the kids when she said, "And no cookies." The boys shoved the table to the back of the stage where it was jerked under the curtain by invisible hands. All but one boy left the stage while Stevi told of the successes and failures of the colony. The remaining boy paced nervously until, with a flourish, Bitsy swept to center stage.

She bowed, then curtsied. She twirled around to the boy and said in a ringing voice, "Doncha wanna tell me sumpin?"

The boy mumbled. Bitsy looked at him in disgust. She turned to the audience and said loudly, "My name's Pacilla and he's sposed to say it for hisself!"

Stevi came quickly to center stage, placing a hand on the shoulder of each child. "And as you can see, John and Priscilla Alden also made their appearance at Plymouth." She herded the children offstage to laughter and applause.

One by one, the children returned to the stage, filling it with pilgrims and Indians. Last on of course was Bitsy, who in grand Tinkerbelle style flitted to the middle of the stage, bowed deeply, and declaimed, "God bless us every one."

~~~

Bitsy's family all went to the café after the performance. Betty handed around cups of cocoa while everyone told Bitsy what a great performance she put on. Mary Nell asked her where she learned the prayer she said at the end. Bitsy looked at her in disbelief. "You know, Grandmary. On TV. Where the little boy throws away his cripple sticks."

Betty's head snapped around. "They're called *crutches*, Bitsy. It's not nice to call them *cripple sticks*."

"Is it as bad as saying *ass*, Mamma?"

"Just about, Bitsy, just about." Betty's color was decidedly pinker as she finished serving everyone.

"Out of the mouths of babes," murmured Walter.

Tommy McCann patted Betty on the hand. "Now you know how it feels." He looked around at the others, "This one could pop some corkers herself."

"Oh, Dad! Nobody wants to hear those old stories."

Sitting down next to Tommy, Buck said quietly, "I do."

~~~

When Rusty and Tommy got home after dropping off Shawna, Tommy stopped Rusty from going to his room with a quick word, "Rusty. I wanna talk to you for a minute."

"OK." Rusty turned back to his dad who motioned him to sit.

"I know you've been wondering what's going on with me. The disappearances, the clearing out of junk food."

"Yeah."

"Well, I've decided I have to get control of my life so I've started going to Overeaters Anonymous."

"OK."

"You're not surprised?"

Rusty's cheeks blazed. "No. I followed you. Today. I saw you and Mr. Keller go into the meeting. Sorry."

"Oh, that's alright." He sighed. "Do you have any questions?"

"No. Yes. I mean. What's it about? Do you go on a diet? Or what?"

Tommy handed Rusty a pamphlet. "Read this. It tells about OA. Then we'll talk."

"OK. But are you, like, a food junkie?"

"It's not that simple. I have problems, but the food is a symptom not the cause. The cause is the way I think. I'm going to work on my thinking and eat three moderate meals a day while I do. No crash diet."

Rusty looked relieved. "Good. That sounds good. I'll read this." He ducked his head and went to his room.

"Betty," he said into the phone after she answered. "Dad told me about OA. He says he has a thinking problem."

~~~

Still chuckling over her granddaughter, Mary Nell picked up Aunt Bess's manuscript. She never remembered her grandmother laughing with her. She took care of her, fed her, made sure she behaved. But she never played. After her mother died and she lived full-time with her grandmother, she only remembered Grandma being sad. She'd try on other emotions, but sadness was her default.

She took a piece of lavender paper to record the details of Edie's baby who came to stay with Bess, Lottie, and Janet. Bess listed the words and phrases the child said, her physical feats of potty training, walking, skipping and playing hop-scotch. Then she found a section that literally stopped her breath:

> Janet's reaction to the child was unpredicted. She took on caring for her as if she were the mother. She encouraged the little girl to call her '"Mamma" and became more and more possessive as time went by.
>
> As for the child, she clung to Janet. After a while her night terrors stopped and she settled into being Janet's adored daughter.
>
> Lottie's interest in the child increased after her initial aloofness and apparent apathy. She fell in love with the little charmer and tried to assist Janet in caring for her. Janet would have none of it. Her mother was barely allowed to hug her grandchild. Janet monitored every move.
>
> But everything worked well enough in the household until the crisis of school attendance. Janet refused to enroll the child in school. If it were even mentioned, she became nearly hysterical. Once, Lottie took her granddaughter to register her only to be defeated by a screaming Janet in the school board office.
>
> Three days after that incident, I finally released my Memphis detective. I had to hire one in Kansas City to find Janet and the child.

....

> Her six weeks absence had taken its toll on Janet. After hospitalization for a lung infection, she was still too ill to return home. The doctors suggested that a change of climate might help Janet's health improve, but she was not strong enough to move to Arizona or Nevada alone. Lottie decided to go with her. In 1961, Lottie, her daughter, and her granddaughter moved to Scottsdale, Arizona.

"I grew up in Scottsdale. My God! I'm Edie's daughter!" She rocked back and forth with the pen in her hand, unable to decide what to write on her piece of lavender paper.

# Chapter 14

Betty called Rusty early on Tuesday morning. "Do you want to see if Shawna can do your Dream Dinner this week. It'll need to be late, after the café is closed. Friday or Saturday."

"Yeah. That'd be good. Thanks. I'll let you know."

"Back in school now? Eye healed?"

"Yeah. Back to normal."

"Oh, I almost forgot. I've been going through stuff Dub left here. It's time I cleared it all out. There's some good cologne, a couple ties, some other stuff. Stop by after school and get it. Now that I've cleared it out, I want it gone."

"OK. Will do. Later."

After getting her chalk, Betty pulled her chalkboard from behind a table and set it on the counter. "Today's Specials" would be grilled chicken with confetti peppers, baked sweet potato, and roasted Brussels sprouts. With Cinnamon Crunch Nut Pie for dessert. She was still writing when the newly installed bell on the door jingled.

"Mornin'. Thought you might want some of this for your diners tonight." Buck held out a box overflowing with baby lettuces. Leaves ranged in color from pale chartreuse through glossy dark green to deep burgundy. Then he set down a smaller box filled with tiny seedlings.

Betty picked up a leaf of spinach, rubbed it between her fingers, and sniffed it before putting it in her mouth. "Wow! Where'd you get all this?"

"Grew it." Buck's eyes sparkled with pleasure. "Lulu helped." He pointed to his best friend sitting on the sidewalk, watching everything that was happening inside the café and out.

"Even the micro-greens?" Betty's eyebrows rose in disbelief.

"Yep. Set up a little hydroponic system in the barn behind the house." He shuffled through the tiny plantlets with one careful finger. "This is mostly broccoli, but there's some arugula in there too."

"Geez. I'm surprised. Astounded, really." She tasted a tiny broccoli seedling. "Nice." She looked Buck up and down, as if seeing him for the first time. "I can't get over it. I'm impressed."

"Impressed enough to buy some of this and order some more?"

"Oh, yeah. You are on, buster. Now you'll have to keep producing you know."

Buck's wide grin curled his crescent moon scar into a capital C. "Plan to. Now you know why I wouldn't tell you my Dream Dinner menu. Wanted to surprise you, bring part of the ingredients."

Betty looked at him carefully. "You can still do that. Bring me what you want cooked."

"Seriously? You got it."

"And in the meantime, how much do you want for these?" she gestured at the boxes.

As they began to negotiate price and future orders, the bell on the door jingled again. Walter Floyd's big grin preceded him in the door. "What are you two up to?"

Between them, Betty and Buck told Walter about Buck's crops and Betty's new supplier.

"I knew about the lettuce, but hydroponics? How'd you learn about that?"

Buck's chest swelled as he said, "Got some books from the library, researched it online, and found a friendly supplier willing to talk. You'll have to see the setup. It's pretty cool."

"And you got it set up in the little barn?"

"Yep."

"Wouldn't somewhere with more natural light be better?"

"Mmm-hmm. But you'd have to be able to shade it. Keep direct sun out."

Walter took out a pen and notepad from his pocket and wrote for a few seconds. "Mary Nell bought the material for a small greenhouse. She's never going to do anything with it. You want it?"

"Sure. I'll figure out something to do with it."

Walter closed his brown eye and squinted at Buck. Then he wrote a few numbers in his little notebook. "Looks to me like there's the beginnin's of a business here. Growin', sellin', and cookin' organic greens, herbs and vegetables. And I want in on it!"

Buck's eyes widened in surprise. Betty looked from one to the other. "I think you're right, Walter."

Walter pointed to a building across the street, "See that yellow building over there? It's almost ready for occupancy. Wouldn't an organic produce market look good there?"

Buck looked stunned. Betty's smile widened.

Walter rocked back on his heels. "We just need to find us someone to manage that store." He turned to Buck, "And to build you a greenhouse and some coldframes."

~ ~ ~

It was early afternoon before Mary Nell could bring herself to face any more shocks. She still was finding it hard to believe. Of course, she'd never known who her father was. Her mother never said, or so her Grandma told her. At least that was probably true.

She took a deep breath and picked up the manuscript. She waded through more of Bess's blasted lists about Janet's illnesses, doctors visited, and travel to and from Arizona. Deaths, births, weddings, divorces, trips taken, trips deferred – all listed. Nearly the last third of the memoirs consisted of lists. But three sections caused her to catch her breath. She copied them onto her colored pages:

> Lottie and her granddaughter stayed in Scottsdale after Janet's death in 1963. Mary Nell was happy in her school and Lottie had made friends there. I went to the funeral, of course, but didn't like the dry heat. I visited seldom.

....

The last time I was in Arizona was at Lottie's funeral in 2004. She outlived her daughter by over forty years. Mary Nell and her family were there. I'd lost touch with her since she went off to college, married, and had children. She was living in Arkansas, not so far in distance from Kansas City, but a world away in time.

I miss Lottie. Not on a daily basis since we had never been very close nor lived together long. But I miss knowing that she's there.

I've tried again to find Edie Campbell Smith. I hired a new detective agency. The trail is definitely cold, but they think that the information available on the internet may actually make it possible to trace her. I have never even seen her face. Yet she haunts me.

....

I just celebrated my one hundredth birthday. I can hardly believe it. And the best present of all was the call I received from the Bates Detective Agency. They located her. After all these years they found Edie Campbell Smith.

But I am too old to carry on. My stamina is gone. My vision, my hearing, my mobility—all gone. I will not follow up. I cannot.

And so it falls to Lottie's daughter's daughter to set things right.

As she reread the final sentence, she remembered a broken prism she used to have. It refracted light in unexpected ways. She just realized that the same could happen with truth.

~~~

Shawna moved her fork closer to the plate. So many utensils. She hoped she was using them correctly. Her mother told her to use them from outside in, but what about the spoon at the top of the placemat? She realized she'd missed whatever Rusty said, so she smiled and nodded. A good substitute for listening sometimes.

Gosh, he was cute tonight. He'd dressed up in a suit and liberally sprinkled on a new cologne. He thanked and praised every course Betty brought out. He talked to Shawna without stuttering. And the food was wonderful. She felt very lucky to be here with Rusty eating this special meal.

Betty served the entrée, "tender slices of pork tenderloin braised in an apricot reduction with garlic mashed potatoes and seasonal vegetables," just like Shawna had written on her Dream Dinner entry. Too bad she couldn't serve them a nice crisp wine.

She stood back and watched while Shawna took the first bite of the pork. "Oh, God. It's so good! When I read about it, I never expected to taste it." Shawna's face glowed.

Betty was pleased that the kids were being so grown up. This was a good idea of Walter's.

She sat at an empty booth, waiting for them to finish that course so she could serve the final two: cheese and fruit, and chocolate soufflé with fresh raspberries and whipped cream. At least they wouldn't leave hungry.

She pulled her sweater over a sleeping Bitsy. It was late for Bits to be out, but she seemed to have no trouble sleeping on the bench of the booth in The Ladies Corner. If Betty was lucky, she'd be able to get Bitsy home without fully waking her. As she smoothed the hair off Bitsy's head, she thought about Mary Nell's call that afternoon.

How could a mother give up her child? She knew Mary Nell always felt motherless, as she did, but at least it was from death not choice. Choice felt much worse. She wondered if missing a parent made Rusty and Shawna closer. She thought it was part of the reason she and Mary Nell had gotten on so well – they knew each other's pain.

She didn't hear silverware still clanking, so she checked on her diners. They had finished and praised the food highly. Betty cleared away their dishes and brought the next course. And finally the desserts. She knew she'd just served these kids the best meal of their lives.

Finally, table cleared, Betty kissed each of them on the cheek and gave them a copy of the menu to take home as a keepsake. She figured Rusty would keep his for a month or so, but Shawna's was destined for a scrapbook.

Rusty said he'd carry Bitsy to the car, so Betty turned off lights as Rusty picked Bitsy up and held her to his shoulder. She put her arms around his neck and murmured, "Oh, Daddy! You came home."

Betty stopped mid-stride. Bitsy hadn't mentioned her dad in months. It must be the cologne Rusty was wearing. He smelled like Dub. Poor Bits. She was another member of the Missing Parents Club.

~~~

Mary Nell was curled into the corner of the sofa, holding a cup of tea when Walter found her. "Aren't you coming to bed yet?" He sat down next to her, placing her feet in his lap.

She looked at him softly. She was at least lucky in her marriage. "Walter, I'm going to have to do it. Try to find her. Aunt Bess said it: it falls to me to set things right."

# Part II:  The Lift

*The lift is the moment of initial contact between the dog and the sheep in which the dog begins moving the sheep to the shepherd*

# Chapter 15

March came in like a lamb this year, Buck thought. At least from a weather perspective. He had a lion's share of work to do, starting at daylight and barely finishing by dark. He and Lulu fell into bed every night and slept like the dead. As an old guy in the hardware store told him, farmers don't have insomnia.

His big greenhouse was filled with all things green and growing. Well, not *all*, he told himself, but many. His expanded hydroponic system created salable micro-greens in just a few days. And he had started some tomatoes, lettuces, and peppers hydroponically, too. He still intended to set out the hot-weather crops into his recently amended and tilled plots as soon as the nights stopped dropping below freezing. His tunnel cold frames protected the cool weather plants like lettuce and broccoli. Next year, he thought he'd try some high tunnels. They'd offer the same protection, but would be easier to work in since you could walk in them and they wouldn't require the daily putting on and taking off of plastic.

And to think he had planned to use a brush row to support his plastic. Things sure had changed since that day in November he took some lettuce to Walter and Mary Nell. He looked around in satisfaction. His plots were tidy and weed-free, or almost, and his cold frames were full.

He sold all he could produce, too. And he'd sell more if he had it. With Walter spreading the word through the organic food network, his orders from local restaurants had doubled. He had even started to hear from as far away as Little Rock and Fayetteville. He needed to talk to Walter about a delivery truck.

Rusty rode up on his bicycle, dismounted, and pitched a ball to Lulu on the way to the greenhouse. He usually got there about three o'clock and worked until six or six-thirty, and all day Saturday. Buck thought he could use him half-days on Sundays, too, beginning in April.

As he picked up Lulu's ball again, Rusty said to Buck, "Sorry I'm late. I had to talk to my lab partner after school about our report that's due tomorrow."

Buck smirked, "Isn't Shawna your lab partner?"

"Umm. You want me to mix fertilizer for the injector system?" Rusty tossed the ball again, avoiding Buck's eye.

"Naw. Already did that. Need you to bump up those Arkansas Travelers from the seed pellets to 7201s. I think they're rooted out enough."

Rusty nodded as he headed into the greenhouse to get started. It was warm inside and smelled like growth. He attached his ipod's earbuds, listened to his favorite tunes, and inserted tiny seedlings grown in pressed peat moss pellets into their new quarters. More room for their roots. He liked potting. He could listen to music and think. Relaxing, really.

Buck clapped him on the shoulder and startled him into a backward leap. "Whoa, there, cowboy." Buck stepped sideways to avoid a collision. "Just wanted to see if you can work some on Sunday. Got a big order of produce to go to the market early Monday for the opening."

"Sure. No problem. What time?" Rusty resumed filling flats that held seventy-two plants each with fine potting soil and poking a pelleted plant into each cell.

"Ten o'clock okay?"

"Yeah. Fine."

Buck left him to his work. He was a good kid. Hard-working and easy to get along with. Good thing Walter coaxed him away from Subway. Good for Rusty, too. Walter paid better.

~~~

*"Tommy McCann's lookin' better. Course he's still got a ways to go."*

*"I heard he was going to Overeaters."*

*"Bernice, over to Dr. Simm's, said she heard the doctor giving Tommy what for. Told him he was killin' himself. Right after that, he started losin' weight."*

*"Good for Doc Sims. You gotta get tough with some of these people."*

Tommy McCann smiled at Shawna as she came into the market and found her apron. "Monday's the big day. You gonna be able to work some extra this weekend to help get ready?"

"Yes, sir. I plan to. It'll be so great to finally get open."

Tommy agreed with her. He'd put in long hours for the last two months to make sure everything would be ready: coolers installed and checked out; signage prepared and hung; suppliers lined up; orders placed. He still didn't know why Walter Floyd convinced him to manage this market, but he was thankful that he had.

Walter stuck his head in the door, "Going to Food King for coffee. Need anything?"

"No, thanks," yelled Shawna from the back. Tommy shook his head.

Looking around at the clean, bright, attractive, well-organized shop, Walter told Tommy, "You've done a great job. All this place needs now is the fresh produce and customers."

Tommy beamed at the praise. "Yep. We're getting' there. It'll be nice to see some dollars comin' in rather than goin' out, huh?"

"Don't worry. It might be slow to start, but word'll get out. You'll have a goin' Jessie on your hands real soon."

"Well, if so, it's thanks to you." Tommy flushed as he spoke, little better at giving praise than receiving it. "But Bitsy may win the prize. Coming up with the name." He pointed at the sign behind the cash register, "Grandpa's Greens."

"She was sure cute that afternoon, wasn't she? Crawlin' up in my lap and saying so seriously, 'You're both Grandpas. Name it after you.' She's somethin'."

Tommy grinned, "She's a corker all right."

Headed out the door, Walter lifted a hand in farewell. "I guess this grandpa better get moving."

Waving back, Tommy looked at the sign again, and chuckled. He surveyed with pride the stainless steel bins, the buffed concrete floors, and the gleaming windows. Then he shook himself and picked up the phone. His custom-printed bags should have been there by now.

~~~

*"What's going on with Mary Nell Floyd? She's been in and out of town like a regular delivery route."*

*"I heard she's lookin' for somebody from her past."*

*"She's not from around here. I don't know where Walter met her."*

*"I heard she's from Arizona."*

*"Didn't they live in Texas for a while?"*

*"Who'd you say she's lookin' for?"*

*"Shhh."*

"Wonder where Mary Nell is now?" Walter mumbled to himself as he drove to Food King. She'd been gone for a week this time, and he missed her. Missed her going to the grocery store, too.

She'd started out with the Bates Detective Agency that Bess had used, but that didn't last long. Once it became clear they had the wrong Edie Smith, things got tense. They talked to her like an old lady, she'd said. And she, by God, was not a lady! Ha! Mary Nell could always make him laugh.

She could have sat back and let the detectives do their work, but that wasn't her style. She met with them and even did a little sleuthing on her own. He was sure that they'd rather she leave that to them, but for what they charged they could damn well do it her way.

He understood her need to find out about her mother. He just wished that she wasn't so single-minded about it. He thought women were supposed to be so good at multi-tasking.

His cell phone rang. He pulled over to the side of the road before he answered it. He didn't see how those kids could drive and talk. Or worse, text.

He saw Mary Nell's name flash on the screen and a small lump of happiness filled his throat as he croaked out his greeting, "Hey, hon. Where are you?"

Mary Nell's voice rang in his ear. She couldn't get used to not yelling into her phone. "Goddam Mississippi. And it's pouring. I can't go look in the cemetery because I lost my damned umbrella. And I left my raincoat at home."

"Other than that, you're having a ball, huh?"

"Oh, sorry. I just don't like having to wait on things. Even the weather. Or maybe, especially the weather. You okay?"

"Fine. On my way to get some coffee at Food King. We're out at home. Seems like I can't remember to buy more than one thing at a time, and if I make a list, I lose it."

"Don't start. I refuse to admit we're getting older and more forgetful. Besides, there's probably some cute young checker you're really going to see."

"Oh, right. So, you got any leads you're following?"

"Not really. Not now. There was a mention of someone named Julia E. Smith in this neighborhood, so I thought I'd look in the cemetery. Gina and Tony at the agency are doing all the records checking, but I couldn't stand sitting around. Not even sure if it's a real lead."

"What's your next step?"

"They're looking for anomalies, things that point to a name change. It's pretty certain she didn't keep her name, but we haven't found record of a change yet. We think we have a lead then hit another dead end. You know, same it's been for three months."

"If it were easy, Bess would have found her years ago."

"I know. But we were so hopeful yesterday, before the bottom fell out."

"Hang in there, hon. When you coming home?"

"Probably Saturday. I'll let you know."

"That'd be good. Grandpa's Greens opens Monday. Be safe. Love you."

"Love you, too." She hung up.

He knew she hated for him to hang up on her, so he always waited. He also knew she'd be back home and back to normal eventually. He could wait for that, too.

# Chapter 16

Monday morning was bright and sunny. From the sidewalk in front of her café, Betty waved at her father across the street. He finished sweeping his sidewalk and turned over the Open sign. Grandpa's Greens was officially open.

As she thought of all the changes in her dad over the past few months, she was astounded again. He had gone from a near recluse to an active, productive citizen of the town.

Last week as she watched him direct people to put this here and that there, Charlie Keller had come in for his afternoon coffee and newspaper. She finally found the courage to approach him.

"Charlie, I don't know what you did to help my dad regain his balance, but whatever it was, thank you!"

Looking up at her from his paper, startled, Charlie quickly cast his eyes back at the article he had been reading. "Aw. I didn't do much. Just offered a little encouragement. And told Tommy my story. He did the rest."

Betty leaned over and squeezed his hand. "You're a good man, Charlie Brown, er Keller." She winked and let him get back to his newspaper. She knew enough from talking to her dad about OA not to ask Charlie about his story. He'd tell it if he wanted to.

Bitsy was at the café today. Her school was closed for teacher's workday. Betty's standby babysitter had a stomach virus, and she hadn't wanted to bother Mary Nell since she had just gotten home from her latest trip. Bits was happily drawing on a paper placemat at the moment. Betty hoped she could stay entertained for a while. Sometimes Bitsy would sit quietly and draw or play with puzzles for hours, and sometimes the Gotta-Moves took control. The worst part was, Betty never new which would strike when.

Bitsy was going through a growth spurt. She'd gained length without weight, and her arms and legs looked like sticks. Her clothes were either too short or fell off her shoulders and hips. She looked like a waif, an orphan.

Funny how often "orphan" came to mind. She guessed a real orphan had neither parent. Wonder what you call somebody with only one parent, besides lonely?

Distracted by her thoughts, Betty nearly missed Bitsy's absence from the counter. When she finally noticed, she felt a stab of fear. She looked around, took a deep breath, and walked back to the restroom. Maybe Bitsy'd needed to go potty. No. Empty.

Back to the kitchen. Had the cook seen Bitsy? No.

Now getting panicky, Betty yelled, "Bitsy. Bitsy! Please come here"

No reply.

Charlie Keller called to her, "Hon, calm down. Look across the street."

Betty turned to look where Charlie pointed and saw Bitsy handing out fliers to passersby under the watchful eye of Tommy McCann. "Deep breath, Betty," she told herself.

As she watched out the window, she saw Mary Nell turn the corner. Bitsy saw her, too. She handed the fliers to Tommy and dashed toward Mary Nell, arms thrown out, shouting at top volume, "Grandmary. Oh, Grandmary! I missed you soooo much!" She threw herself at Mary Nell, nearly tripping her. Mary Nell bent to engulf Bitsy in her arms as she returned the enthusiastic hug.

Finally releasing Bitsy, Mary Nell took her hand, swinging it as they walked, "I hoped I'd find you. After I look over your Grandpa's store, I'm gonna ask your mamma if you can come home with me. I have something at my house with your name on it."

Eyebrows drawn together, Bitsy said, "Grandmary. There's lots of things at your house with my name on them. All my books I left there, and my old backpack, and…."

"Hmm-hmm. I know Bits. But I meant I have a present for you."

"You do? Oh, Grandmary! Wait 'til I tell Mamma!"

~~~

A day with Bitsy was good for Mary Nell's soul. She needed exuberance and delight. Bitsy provided both, in spades. She was ecstatic about the Gone with the Wind doll Mary Nell had found.

"Did little girls dress like this in olden times, Grandmary? How did they get all these clothes on? How did they button the back of their dress? How did they go potty?"

Mary Nell patiently answered question after question. Each response triggered more questions. Then, as she should have expected, Bitsy declared that she *needed* a dress like Scarlett's.

Only hers should be green not blue. Finally, after dancing and curtsying in her pretend dress, Bitsy began to wear down.

"Why don't you and Scarlett curl up on the couch while I go make us some lunch."

"OK, Grandmary. Scarlett wants peanut butter and banana." She climbed on the couch, lay back, and began singing something to Scarlett about too many buttons.

While making lunch, Mary Nell was nearly knocked over by a tidal wave of sadness. How could someone abandon a child like Bitsy? How could her mother abandon *her*? She shook herself and said sternly, "Well you can stay in here feeling sorry for yourself or you can go enjoy your granddaughter." And with that stern self-admonishment, she put together a peanut butter and banana sandwich.

She cut the sandwich in two and placed one half on a small plate. The other half, she cut in eighths and placed one of the tiny pieces on a little china plate originally designed to hold a butter pat. She poured a glass of milk and also filled a tiny teacup. Carrying them to the table, she set two places, and called to Bitsy, "Come to the table, Bitsy. And bring Scarlett. Her lunch is ready."

Bitsy scampered in with Scarlett. When she saw the table, she threw her arms out, "Oh! Grandmary!"

~~~

Buck sat at the counter in the café and watched the traffic at Grandpa's Greens across the street. He was tired. He'd been up since four-thirty that morning picking, packaging and delivering his harvest. It looked like their work would pay off. He loved to see his greens exit the store in bag after bag.

Now that the start-up work was done, he knew the work wouldn't stop but should settle into a routine. Working hard wasn't a problem, but the uncertainties of starting from scratch fueled his Tums habit. He and Lulu needed a little break. After Rusty got to the greenhouse this afternoon, he thought he'd take Lulu to the river for a bout of ball throwing and chilling out.

"Proud?" Betty asked as she refilled his coffee cup, noticing him watch every move across the street.

"Yep. Of Rusty and Tommy, too. They've been great."

"I come from good stock," Betty deadpanned.

Coffee sprayed with a "Pffaa." Buck struggled to stifle a laugh. "Guess you do."

"Speaking of stock, has Walter found anybody else to help with the cattle and chickens?"

"Think so. Saw him walking some guy around the cattle barn. Tell you the truth, hardly had time to think of it. Walter told me weeks ago not to worry about 'em, and I haven't. Spent all my time plantin', pickin', pottin' or prunin'."

"I thought it was too early to prune."

"You know what I mean. Smart ass."

"That reminds me. I thought you were gonna bring me ingredients to cook you a dinner. Seems like a good time to do it. Grand opening of Grandpa's Greens."

"Almost forgot about that. How about this weekend?"

"You bring it, I'll cook it."

"OK. Gotta be in town every day this week anyway 'til we figure out restocking schedules. Bring the groceries toward the end of the week."

He left after a few more minutes of watching the activities across the street.

He was a puzzle. A redneck gourmet. Wonder what he'd bring her to cook.

~~~

*"Looks like Grandpa's Greens is gonna be a success. People lined up at the check-out counter."*

*"You been in there yet? They got good prices. I figgered they'd be higher'n a cat's back, all that organic stuff. But looked pretty reasonable. And fresh."*

*"I saw that Myrna Tyree in there. She still all lovey-dovey with the Rev?"*

*"I heard there's trouble in paradise."*

*"Wouldn't surprise me none. Saw her flirtin' with that cowboy, Buck. Hell, she could be his mother."*

*"Maybe she is. Heard she'd sprinkled kids around three counties."*

After school, Shawna hurried to the store. She couldn't wait to see how the first day had gone. Even though she only worked there part time, she felt like she'd made a contribution to the store. She'd come up with the idea of the recipe bag – a bag filled with the fresh ingredients to prepare the recipe included.

Her first version was Vegetable Soup. She got the recipe from Betty, then bagged the right vegetables together in a recyclable bag and tied a wooden spoon on top. Wonder if they sold any.

"Hey, Shawna," Tommy greeted her grinning. "This has been a helluva day. We've been swamped since the door opened. And we sold every one of your recipe bags. Can you put some more together for tomorrow?"

"Yes!" She pumped her fist in the air. She bounced into the back room to assemble more vegetable soup bags. Maybe she could do some different ones, too, as the season progressed. Salad bags and pasta primavera bags and Chinese wok bags! She lost track of time as she assembled and planned. She thought she'd ask Mr. Floyd if they could carry bulk organic rice and pasta. Then she could add those to her creations. He was easy to talk to. Listened to her and didn't make her feel like a kid.

Rusty was picking her up tonight and taking her for pizza. They would celebrate opening day. She found herself depending on Rusty more and more. He might have been a slow starter but he was a keeper.

# Chapter 17

Looking at her email folder was a lot like wishing on a star, Mary Nell thought. She only looked to see if anything new from Gina or Tony had come in. She had hired them after good recommendations from a couple of Walter's friends, but she didn't know whether Edie was an exceptionally good hider or Tony and Gina weren't very good finders. In her more cynical moments, she wondered if they were stringing her along, throwing out little crumbs, but all the while heading deeper into the forest of never-ending retainers.

She did know that she was weary. Weary of wondering, weary of self-blame, weary of anger. But anger kept depression at bay, so she let her level rise and directed it at that smarmy jackass, Billy J. Yeats. How he convinced Bess to play that silly game of thirty-days' delay for reading the memoirs, she wasn't sure. But that sort of sadism was not Bess Campbell's style. At least the will was straight-forward: half to Mary Nell and half to Edie. Edie's share would be held in trust until she was found or found to be legally dead.

Actually the only surprise in the will had been the extent of the estate. Bess lived very frugally, invested wisely, and built up substantial holdings. One of Mary Nell's topics for 2:00 a.m. worrying was what to do with that estate. Even half, assuming she could find Edie, was large.

She continued to look at the list of messages in her email. Damn. An email from Yeats just came in. He wanted to meet with her to

sign papers about probating the will and to present his expense
statement. She'd let him call her. And make him explain every
penny he charged her. If only she hadn't let Walter talk her into
keeping him on until the will was probated, she could fire that
slimy lizard with such satisfaction.

As she let her anger build, her need to act increased
proportionally. She had jumped out of the chair and headed out
of the room when her computer beeped a "you've got mail"
alarm. She hesitated, then went back to look.

"Tethered", she thought. "I let myself be the tetherball of email."
She opened the email from Gina thinking it was probably a
request for more money. Bess's estate could well afford the
expense, but how much longer would she able to emotionally
afford it? How did Bess do this for so many years? "Oh, Hell!
Read it and be done," she said loudly as she opened the message:

> We have a strong lead in Plainview, OK. Tony's gone
> there to validate. We'll let you know what we find. Keep
> your fingers crossed. Gina

Mary Nell caught her breath, stood up, and paced through the
dining room, kitchen, and hall. She grabbed a jacket and headed
out the door, then turned around to find her cell phone and put
it in her pocket. "Walk," she said. "I'll walk."

After a few minutes of brisk walking, she felt a cold nose bump
into her hand. She was surprised to find herself at the
greenhouse with Lulu by her side. Lulu dropped a ball at her feet,
wanting a play partner. Mary Nell complied, throwing it high just
to watch Lulu leap in the air and twist to catch the ball. Lulu was
proud of her flying leaps, and roo-roo'ed her pleasure when she
returned the ball.

She made Mary Nell laugh out loud with one particularly operatic
display. She was pounding Lulu's sides and telling her what a
great dog she was when Buck ambled out.

"Thought I saw somebody out here. Lulu con you into playing with her?"

"Oh, it's a pleasure. She's a great dog. Where'd you get her anyway?"

"Over in Oklahoma. Plainview. Funny kennel name – can't think of if right now. Run by some women. One named Belle, I think. Breeds and trains border collies and bloodhounds. Says other dogs can herd or track, but she only wanted specialists. Funny old gal. Liked her. Why? You want a pup?"

"When I'm with Lulu I do. I miss having a dog, and Walter wouldn't care. I don't know. Maybe it's time." She threw the ball again for Lulu. "Did you say Plainview?"

"Yep. Been there? Ain't much to remember."

"No, I haven't been there. Hadn't even heard of it 'til today. Now I heard of it twice. Odd."

"Synchronicity. Or just coincidence." He rubbed his neck, "Hmm. Probably a good place to hide."

"What is?"

"Plainview. *Purloined Letter* and all that."

"Cute." She rolled her eyes at him. "Where is it?"

"Out in the middle of Nobody Cares. On the Kansas border almost to the Panhandle."

"You go there special for the dog?"

"Naw. Happened on it. Headed west out of Ponca City and ran into Plainview looking for another little place. Hooker." He winked, whistled for Lulu and went back into the greenhouse.

Mary Nell chuckled, "Bet you were, cowboy. Adios." She turned toward home, her spirits improved. Buck was a curiosity, all right.

~~~

Tommy directed Rusty and Shawna where to place the cartons of lettuce Rusty had just delivered. He told Rusty to carry everything into the store and follow Shawna's lead – the girl, at least, had a head on her shoulders.

Looking at his dad with amusement, Rusty forced a scowl on his amiable face, "Listen here now, Dad. If you keep workin' me like this, I'm gonna tell Mr. Floyd to take my pay out of the retail budget rather than the production one."

Tommy laughed at his son's attempt at acting. "Go ahead. Make my day!" He slapped Rusty on the back as he bent to change the prices for the new shipment. He lowered the price on the lettuce. Production costs had dropped as warmer weather lowered the heating requirements.

Shawna's expression softened as she watched Rusty and his dad. Rusty had talked about his dad at dinner last night. He said Tommy was acting more like he used to, before Rusty's mother died – full of fun, teasing, and laughter. She understood what death did to a family. Luckily her mother hadn't crashed so hard.

She and Rusty talked about everything now that he'd conquered his wobbles. Last night she'd asked him if she was anything like his mother. He got very quiet, rubbed the side of his neck with his left hand and closed his eyes.

Finally, he looked at her and nodded. "Yeah, some. She was about your size, and her hair was a similar color – a little lighter. And you look at me the way she did sometimes. Your face gets soft and the corners of your eyes squint up. Why?"

"Just wondered. I read something about how kids who lose a parent look for the missing parent in other people – teachers, friends, people they go out with or marry."

"Hmm. So do I remind you of your dad?"

She grimaced, "I've been trying to figure that out. You don't look anything like him. He was taller, heavier, blonde. But you listen like he did. And you're honest about yourself, like he was. I see some of his strengths in you."

"That's flattering. What about his weaknesses?"

"He had a quick temper and a sharp tongue. He said he had to keep working on that, or he'd spend all his time apologizing for mouthing off. He learned things quickly and was impatient with people he thought weren't trying. He tried not to show it, but I could tell when he wanted to just do the thing himself rather than wait on a beginner." She took a deep breath. "I don't see that in you. You don't get angry easily or lose patience with people quickly. You're careful with your words."

"Mmm-hmm. Probably too much. I should speak up way before I do. I never did say anything to Dad about his eating."

"Rusty, that's not your fault," she squeezed his hand. "Try not to blame yourself for things you can't control. You know the Serenity Prayer?"

Rusty shook his head.

"Ask your dad. I bet he'd like to tell you about it."

Rusty nodded, "OK. I will." He sat up straighter, "And now Ms. Taylor, can we talk about something lighter? Like helium. I think we ought to get some balloons for the Grand Opening party on Saturday. Maybe use them for people to win prizes with somehow. Whacha think?"

"Yeah. You could put something inside the balloons, and people could bust them to get it out. A toy or candy or mmm, something."

Rusty rubbed the side of his neck with his hand again. "Yeah. Maybe. Something to save them money. A coupon for the store or another business. Like the Food King giving cents off for a gallon of gas at the Gas Island."

A big grin spread across Shawna's face. "I know. Let's print up some coupons to put inside the balloons with cents off gasoline on one side. And the other could say 'Grandpa's Greens Give you Gas!'."

Shawna shook herself back to the present, unloading lettuce. Then she giggled. Maybe she really would make up a special balloon coupon just for Rusty.

~~~

*"That Walter Floyd's sure been busy. I hear he owns most of Blue Fork."*

*"Twelve buildings on Main Street, I heard."*

*"His family from over in Yell County?"*

*"Think so. Never heard any of the Floyds had two nickels to rub together 'cept for Walter."*

Walter had been gone all day, up in Benton County, dealing with a potential buyer of a strip mall he had developed. He had lost interest in renting small retail spaces except in Blue Fork. His latest venture with Buck and Tommy reaffirmed his decision to get more involved, hands-on involved, in his own town. He'd put a very attractive price on the Benton Country property. He'd do the same for the others. He found himself humming the Kenny Rogers' song with some of his favorite lyrics, "You've got to know when to hold 'em, know when to fold 'em, know when to walk away, know when to run." It wasn't running time yet, but it soon would be.

He drove slowly through town just before dark. Tommy was still in Grandpa's Greens waiting on a late customer. Betty's window tables were full. Other shops had turned on their outside lights so the business district glowed like Christmas to Walter's eyes.

As he drove past the greenhouse, he saw Rusty, Buck and Lulu closing up the cold frames. The blue glow from the grow-lights in the big greenhouse made Rusty and Buck look like the walking dead.

Just then the moon peeked from behind a cloud. Its light reflected from the expanses of plastic covering the cold frames and greenhouse, changing the scene from a horror movie to a sci-fi flick about an outpost on Mars. Walter chuckled at himself, "You're getting fanciful, old man."

As he pulled in front of his house, he was disappointed to see no lights on. Mary Nell was either gone again or holed up in front of the computer in her office. He suspected the latter. She was so wound up over the search for her mother, he worried for her.

He got out of the car and stopped to listen—was that Mary Nell calling? Yep, she was calling the cat, "Berta, Roberta! Berta, Roberta!" The beam from her flashlight preceded her from the back of the house, around the roses, and toward him.

"Hey!" she greeted him. "Have you seen Roberta?"

"No, but I just drove up. How long has she been gone?"

"I'm not sure when I saw her last. I know I haven't seen her all afternoon. I need to find her!"

"She's a cat, hon. She can take care of herself."

"Walter, I need to find her. Are you going to help or stand there spouting platitudes?" Hands on hips, Mary Nell struggled to control her anger.

"OK, OK. Were you in any of the outbuildings today?"

"Yeah. I went into the tractor shed to find some trash bags. I'm sure I closed the door. Oh, God! Maybe I shut her in."

"We'll know in a minute. Give me the flashlight. I'll go check."

"No, I'm going too. I hope she's okay." She sounded so distraught that Walter put his arm around her waist as they walked to the shed.

"Point the light at the lock, hon."

She held the light for him but called steadily, "Berta, Roberta! Berta, Roberta!"

Walter flipped the latch and pushed open the door. Green eyes looked up at them, accompanied by an angry "Myeew!"

Mary Nell bent to pick up Roberta as a tear spilled down her cheek and glinted in the flashlight beam. She held the cat and nuzzled her neck. Walter watched her carefully. He put his arm back around her waist as they walked to the house. "This isn't all about Roberta, is it?" He felt her head shake. "What happened?"

"Got an email. They think they found her out in Oklahoma. I'm going Frickin' Nuts waiting. Then I couldn't find Berta. I nearly lost it. I'm glad you're home. Saved me a trip to the loony bin."

He squeezed her to him, "I can still take you."

~ ~ ~

For once, Betty had to fight Bitsy about getting ready for bed. "Just a minute, Mamma. I'm almost done."

"You told me that ten minutes ago. What are you doing that can't wait 'til morning? Come on now."

Bitsy stuck her head into the living room where Betty was working on her bills and receipts. Bitsy said loudly, "Now presenting Scarlett and Bitsy!" She bounced into the room carrying Scarlett and wrapped in the curtains from her bedroom window. Scarlet was in the valance.

Betty stared at her for a long moment then burst into laughter. She hugged Bitsy and Scarlett and walked them to bedroom. She needed to talk to Mary Nell about those *Gone with the Wind* stories.

# Chapter 18

Buck stopped in the café on Friday morning and dropped off the ingredients for the dinner Betty promised to cook. He had arugula and beet micro-greens, fresh mussels, baby lettuces, a Cherokee purple tomato, baby carrots, baby broccoli, and three quail.

Betty looked on with approval as he lay all his offering on the counter. "You must be starved. There's a lot of food here."

"Not too much for two," he replied with a wink.

"Oh. Bringing a guest?"

He thought he heard a hint of disappointment in her voice. "Thought you'd eat with me. Shame for you to cook it all and not eat it."

"Hmm. We'll see. Dinner at 9:30? I know it's late, but I'll need a little time to finish things up after the café closes."

Buck nodded. "9:30. I'll get wine."

Betty waved as he left, already planning how to cook the quail. There was a recipe she'd wanted to try that she'd tucked away for the right time. And what could she do for dessert?

~~~

*"Did you see Buck Toomey carryin' in a bunch of grocery sacks at the café this mornin'? Wonder what that's about?"*

*"He's pretty nice lookin'. Maybe Betty's got her eye on him?"*

*"Shh! She'll hear you."*

*"Well maybe she should. Everybody in town'll be talkin'."*

Pacing, looking at the computer for new email, pacing, sitting and pretending to read, Mary Nell managed to hold herself together until ten o'clock that morning. Then unable to think of anything else to do, she phoned Betty. "Busy?"

"Not at the moment. Breakfast crowd's gone. I'm looking at recipes. What's up?"

"I'm going stark ravers. I'm not a good waiter. Good at waiting, I mean."

"What're you waiting for?" She continued to flip through her card file as she talked.

"Word about whether the lead Gina and Tony found is real. And I'm not sure what outcome to hope for."

"Yeah, you are. You're just nervous."

"Ahh, guess so. Anyway. Okay if I pick up Bits after school? If anything can keep my mind off waiting, she can. She could occupy Northern France."

"Ha! Sure. You want her for the night? I'm cooking a late dinner for Buck, and she'd be asleep before we're done."

"Late dinner for Buck, huh? Woo-woo. I'd love to have Bitsy overnight. I'll pick her up at school. Thanks. Have fun with Bucky."

"Mary Nell, you stop that. You're jumping…." She realized she was speaking to dead air. Mary Nell always hung up first.

Mary Nell almost called Walter to ask him to pick up something for supper when she remembered that she could get her email at the South Pole with her Blackberry. God, she was rattled. The knot in her stomach was getting worse. "OK, Mary Nell. Do something constructive and imaginative." She walked into Bitsy's room and looked around. What could she do to enchant her granddaughter? What had she liked to do at five?

That was a problem. She couldn't remember herself at five. Wasn't that when they moved to Scottsdale? Mamma was sick. Er, Aunt Janet. She had put up pieces of paper on an empty wall and let me draw. Grandma got me some paint.

Mary Nell shook her head to clear it before climbing to the attic. She was sure that there was an easel up there that had been Jif's. Dub wouldn't play with anything that didn't involve a ball, but Jif liked to paint. Jif. Another subject to avoid. In the Air Force in Kuwait. "Safe," he said. Right.

She walked to a spot above Jif's old room. Yep. There it was next to the telescope. She was proud of her attic organization: everything above where it was used.

She hauled the easel down the stairs, cleaned it up and looked for a place to put it. Somewhere washable and paint proof. The breakfast nook would work – tile floors and washable walls. She took the table and chairs to the garage and set up the easel in the middle of the space.

Next a smock. She found one of Walter's old shirts, cut off the sleeves, and decorated it with some acrylic paint she found in the garage. She could stop and get some tempera paints on the way to pick up Bitsy. By the time she had everything arranged, it was time to go.

She bought paints, paper and brushes, then got fixings for a pizza and fruit for snacks. She surprised Bitsy at school, and drove them to the farm accompanied by Bitsy's happy chatter.

Mary Nell said nothing about her surprise, just went into the kitchen to fix a snack. "Bitsy. Snack time."

Bitsy rounded the corner from the hall and stopped in front of the breakfast nook. "Grandmary, there's no place to sit."

"Sit here" Mary Nell said as she patted the seat of a stool at the counter. She had cut up a banana, an apple and an orange on the cutting board. Next she assembled the snack – two banana slices in the middle of the saucer, an orange slice curving above each, and an apple wedge with the red skin to the bottom centered under the banana slices. She placed the dish in front of Bitsy.

"Oh, Grandmary! It's a fruit face!" She smiled hugely, threw her arms wide, and exclaimed, "I love you, Grandmary!"

Mary Nell smoothed Bitsy's cheek, "I love you, too, punkin."

Bitsy took a slice of orange in each hand, dancing them across the counter-top, singing an orange song with words accompanying bounces on the counter top. "Orange, orange, orange. Ju-ju-ju. Orange, orange, orange. Juice!" With the final syllable, she popped the slice into her mouth. After the second slice met the same fate, she looked seriously at the remaining fruit.

"It's another song, Grandmary! Ay-ples and Ba-Nay-Nays. You know that one?" And she sang, ignoring most of the lyrics except for Ee-ples and Ba-Nee-Nees, Oh-ples and Ba-No-Nos, and Uples and Ba-Nu-Nus, taking tiny bites of the appropriate fruit with each verse.

After she finished her milk, Bitsy hopped down from the stool and went back to the breakfast nook. She pointed at the easel, "What's this thing doing here?"

"It's for you. Look!" Mary Nell got out the paints and brushes, put the pad on the easel, and pulled out the smock for Bitsy's examination.

Mary Nell pointed out the painted stars and suns and flowers decorating the old shirt and earned a loud "Oh, Grandmary!"

"You've painted before, haven't you?"

"No, Grandmary."

"Well, just try it. There's lots of paper and paint. Experiment."

Bitsy reached for a brush from the red paint and drew a big circle. She took the brush from the black paint and dotted in eyes. A slash of orange for a mouth. Then blue spikes around the outside. "I'm done, Grandmary."

Mary Nell took the page off the pad and got the push pins. "Let me put this up and I'll help you take off your smock."

"No, Grandmary. I hafta spearmint." She put a stripe of blue at the top of the clean page.

"Is that sky, Bits?"

Bitsy shook her head, "Pay tenshun, Grandmary. You'll see."

Mary Nell did see. She saw Bitsy complete seven paintings before she declared she had to quit because Roberta was probably hungry. Mary Nell agreed, helped her de-smock and feed the cat.

"Boy, Bitsy, Gramps is gonna be surprised at all these paintings you made."

"Grandmary," Bitsy turned to look at her with eyes widened, "I just *tried*."

After Bitsy was in bed, Mary Nell recounted Bitsy's afternoon activity to Walter. "You know, it's criminal that she had never painted before. Doesn't that school have an art program?"

"I don't know, hon, but I bet you're going to find out."

"I'm gonna try."

"You and Bitsy. Just try!" Walter patted her head on the way out of the room. "Going to bed. Coming?"

"In a minute." She walked back into the kitchen and looked at the eight paintings hanging on the wall. "Thank you for getting me through this day," she said softly before turning off the light.

~~~

Buck arrived at the café a few minutes after nine o'clock that night. The aromas of garlic and roasting meat hit him in the salivary glands. He hoped he wouldn't drool.

Betty looked him up and down. "You clean up good." He had on khaki slacks and a blue long-sleeved shirt with open neck and rolled cuffs. "First time I've ever seen you out of jeans." He waggled his eyebrows at her. "I mean, in different clothes," dark pink crept up her cheeks.

"Thought I'd better dress to fit the occasion. Whatever you've done with my food, it smells great."

She nodded her thanks and began to set the first course on the table. He was pleased to see that she'd set two places. He really wanted to talk with her. He had things to tell her.

Finally they sat to eat. The cup of delicately flavored asparagus soup she served first was delicious. He tasted it like it was wine, rolling it around his mouth. Swallowing it, he asked, "Allspice?"

"Damn. I thought that was my secret ingredient." She cleared away the small bowls, and set the next course in front of him, then joined him to eat it. Course after course, Buck ate with relish. His comments were apt and accurate. Betty studied him throughout the meal, asking herself again, "Who is this guy?"

With the amaretto soufflé, Buck started to fidget. It was time. He straightened his shoulders, took a deep breath, rubbed his palms down his thighs, and started. "Betty, I want to talk to you about something. I like you…."

She was quick to jump in, "I like you, too, Buck. But I'm not…."

"Wait. I really need to say this. Please?" He took another deep breath as she gave a hesitant nod. "I'm not who you think I am."

Betty frowned, "What do you mean?"

He held up his hand, palm outward. "Wait." Breathe, Buck, breathe. "I was a rodeo cowboy. Calf roper. Bull rider. Tough, wild. Drank too much, partied too hard, married too young, cheated too often. Woke up too many mornings next to a stranger.

"Then about eight years ago I got hurt." He touched his scar. "Bad hurt. Spent some time in the hospital in Tulsa. Realized I had to do something else. Couldn't keep getting thrown off bulls. Getting too old. Needed a job. Took the first one I saw, at a restaurant across the street from the hospital. Dishwasher. Got to know the chef, Dana Champion. Got my head on, went back to school."

He paused, took a sip of coffee, rubbed his left palm on his slacks and drew another deep breath. "Got close to Dana." He studied Betty. She nodded. "We opened a restaurant, Champions. Dana ran the kitchen. I did everything else." He sipped his coffee.

"I've heard of it," Betty said quietly.

Buck nodded. Another sip. "Things were good. Then Dana got sick. Pancreatic cancer." Another sip. Deep breath. "Quick."

Betty sat immobile. She saw the pools in his lower eyelids and said nothing. She closed her eyes and took several slow breaths. When she opened them again, Buck had wiped his eyes and put on a stony mask.

He spoke woodenly, "Couldn't stay there. Couldn't be, um, restaurant manager, owner, whatever. Sold the place. Found my old boots cleaning out the house. Thought why not? Be again who I was before.

"Put the house up for sale, threw some clothes in a box, put Lulu in the truck, and headed to the Ozarks. Lived around here for a while when I was a kid."

He looked around the café, smiled slightly, "Stopped here for coffee. You sent me to Walter." He shrugged. "You know the rest."

Betty looked him in the eye and nodded slightly. "Thanks," she said softly. She felt the familiar sting of tears forming. She quickly stood and fetched the coffee pot. He didn't need sympathy, but he did need more coffee.

# Chapter 19

*"Buck stayed in town late last night."*

*"Bet he didn't go hungry."*

*"Toomey? Weren't there Toomey's over in St. John?"*

*"Yeah. Haven't heard of 'em lately though. Years ago there was that kid ran off and left his wife. Wasn't she pregnant, too."*

Bitsy woke up and jumped out of bed and ran to see where her grandparents were. Walter, reading the paper, was surprised when the page collapsed into his chest followed by a giggle. "Mornin' Gramps. I'm hungry. Fix me some bunny cakes? Please."

Walter hugged Bitsy. "OK, Sunshine. Bunny cakes it is." He pulled out flour, buttermilk, eggs, baking powder, baking soda and salt. He set the griddle on the burner and rubbed it with a stick of butter. A few minutes later, he preparing his specialty, a pancake in the shape of a bunny.

From the stool beside him, Bitsy directed him in the proper formation of ears, "Make it longer, Gramps. He needs to hear."

After she delivered the pancakes to the table, Bitsy yelled, "Grandmary. The bunnies are ready."

Mary Nell set down her Blackberry and came to the table, In answer to an inquiring look from Walter, she shook her head.

Then turning her attention to Bitsy, she asked, "Is one of these for me?"

Bitsy nodded. "Yes, Grandmary. The one with the broke ear."

Mary Nell took the indicated bunny from the platter. "Which one's yours, Bits?"

"Long ears." She pointed.

"And Gramps?"

"That one." It looked more like a cat than a rabbit.

Mary Nell looked questioningly at Walter. He shrugged, "Ran out of batter." He served up the pancakes and offered around the syrup.

Bitsy told a roundabout story of a rabbit hopping through the forest as they ate. Mary Nell and Walter were trying valiantly to contain their laughter when Mary Nell's Blackberry rang.

She looked at the caller ID, and announced, "Gina."

She picked up the phone, walked to her office, and answered, "Hi, Gina."

Walter watched her depart, saying softly to himself, "Let it be okay."

"Hi, Mary Nell. Let me get Tony on with us. Hold on."

"Hi, Mary Nell." Tony joined the call. "I've got news. We've found her. She's in Plainview, Oklahoma. She's lived there for years under another name. But I am one hundred percent positive she started out life as Julia Edith Campbell. Do you want us to approach her?"

"No. I'll do it." Calming breath, she said to herself, then continued, "Thank you both. I'm in shock. I can't even think. Send me her contact information, please. I'll figure out what to do next. Right now, I need to go." She disconnected and sat staring at the phone.

Bitsy came in, climbed into her lap, and said, "Did the blueberry phone tell you bad things?"

"No, Bits. I think it's good news. I just have to figure out what to do about it."

"You can do it, Grandmary. Just try."

~~~

Rusty and Shawna had fun creating coupons for the Grand Opening Balloons. "Grandpa's Greens help you see better" on the front side offered a free bunch of carrots on the back. "Grandpa's Greens help you smell better" flipped to a coupon for a free bunch of lavender. "Grandpa's Greens keep the doctor away" got you apples. All together, they created twenty different coupons. And Shawna created one special one for Rusty.

Saturday morning found them stuffing the coupons into balloons, filling them with helium, and tying on strings. They tied them in bouquets above each bin of produce. Rusty hung the sign that proclaimed in multiple colors: "Pop a Balloon and See What You've Won!"

They were proud of their idea and its execution. Tommy and Walter had also been enthusiastic. Now they didn't have to wait long before they'd see how the customers reacted.

Buck brought in the last load of vegetables, Tommy straightened the displays, and Rusty and Shawna finished up the balloons.

Walter arrived, looked around, broke into a big grin and yelled, "Wooo-hooo! This place looks great. Thanks everybody! We're gonna have us a helluva party!"

He linked elbows with Shawna and do-si-doed her around the cabbage bin. They were all laughing at the high spirits when they heard a knock at the door.

Tommy unlocked the door to one of The Ladies. She nodded stiffly, and with pursed lips, looked at the sign and then the balloons. She asked Tommy if she had to buy something to pop a balloon.

As he pulled a bouquet of balloons toward her, Tommy said, "Of course not. Have a balloon."

She looked them over carefully, then chose a red one with a black dot in the middle. Shawna gasped, but stood as if frozen.

Tommy picked up a long pin and popped the chosen balloon. He picked up the coupon and held it up for his customer to read. She looked at it for a moment, stiffened her spine, spat out, "Well, I never," and left.

Tommy, Walter, and Rusty looked at Shawna's blanched face, then Tommy read the coupon. "Grandpa's Greens give you Gas." Hoots of laughter echoed through the room.

Shawna said weakly, "It was supposed to be for Rusty," starting a fresh round of hilarity.

~~~

*"It said what?"*

*"I'm not repeating it again."*

*"Well, I never."*

*"Crass, I say."*

*"It didn't hurt their business, though. Lines out the door all day."*

*"I just can't believe that nice Tommy McCann would do that."*

*"I heard it was that Taylor girl."*

*"Well, what would you expect. Her mamma's no better than she should be."*

~~~

The next time Mary Nell checked, Gina's email had arrived. Her mouth got dry as she opened the message. It was short and to the point:

> Here it is, Mary Nell. Good luck. Let us know
> how we can help.
>
> Gina
>
> Belle Sheppard
> BellWhether Kennels
> Box 7
> Plainview, OK 73842
> 580-843-3647
> belle@bellwhether.com

Such a wealth of information in such a few words, Mary Nell thought. She looked at it again. My God. Wasn't that where Buck got Lulu? She had to find Buck.

~~~

*"Did you see Mary Nell Floyd come barrelin' into Grandpa's Greens lookin' for Buck? She looked half crazy."*

*"Told you she's after that cowboy."*

*"Naw. She looked more scared than anything."*

*"I saw her 'bout throw Bitsy into the café before she ran across the street."*

*"Somethin's got to her."*

Buck was helping out at Grandpa's Greens, carrying out packages and being agreeable when Mary Nell flew in.

"Thank God! I've been looking everywhere for you," she panted.

Buck looked up surprised. "Me? Why? You OK? Betty? Bitsy?"

"Oh, sorry. Everyone's fine. I just got a bee in my bonnet and I had to find out. So I've been chasing all over town trying to find you."

"Find out what?" Buck looked at her like she'd sprouted a third eye.

She inhaled and exhaled slowly. "I know I must look like a lunatic. All I want to know is where you told me you got Lulu."

"Out in Oklahoma. Plainview. Why?"

She stared at him for a minute, then blinked and tried to focus, blowing through her mouth with a whoof. "It's a long story. Short version. I've been looking for someone from my past. Turns out she changed her name to Belle Sheppard and now runs BellWhether Kennels in Plainview, Oklahoma. I thought that was where you told me you got Lulu. And I just had to know."

"OK?" He looked a question at her, clearly thinking she'd tipped over the edge.

Mary Nell shook her head. "I think I'm in shock." She rubbed her left temple then continued, "Didn't you say something about the *Purloined Letter* that day?"

"I was being a smart ass. I said Plainview was a good place to hide something. Like in the *Purloined Letter.*"

Mary Nell nodded in silence, her eyes looking into the distance. After a few seconds, she turned back to him, "Thanks, Buck." She started to walk away, muttering under her breath, "Hidden in Plainview all these years."

Back at home, Mary Nell stared at her computer. She had decided the least intrusive way to contact Belle Sheppard was to write a letter. The problem was that she had nothing to say. Or too much to say and no way to say it.

Her thoughts were in such a jumble. If she could organize them she'd have a way to start. She dug through the stacks of papers she'd put away after completing her study of Bess's manuscript and found a pad of blank ivory pages. These would do.

She headed one page FACTS. On it she wrote "Julia Edith Campbell, Born: March 23, 1939." Under that, she wrote the contact information for Belle Sheppard that Gina had sent her.

On another sheet, she wrote SUPPOSITIONS. Here she listed adoption, name change, abandoned daughter. Below that she added in heavy script, "MY MOTHER?"

A third piece of paper she headed FEELINGS. She chewed her lip for a minute, then started writing quickly: "lost, afraid, angry, abandoned, unworthy, guilty. Hoodwinked. Lied to. Fear of further abandonment, rejection. Afraid she's the wrong person. Afraid she's the right one. Angry. Why didn't they tell me my mother's alive? Betrayed."

She wrote and wrote, everything that came to mind. Tears stained some of the pages, but still she wrote. She covered five pages, writing furiously, quickly, jabbing the pen into the paper.

When she finished, she sat back and hugged herself, calmed herself. She concentrated on her breathing. After a few minutes, she went to the kitchen for a cup of tea. She was wrung out. Parched. Exhausted. As she waited for the water to heat, she looked around at Bitsy's paintings still in the breakfast nook and felt a nudge of joy. A thin smile played at her lips. "WWBD. What would Bitsy do?" But she knew.

# Chapter 20

After a sleepless night, Mary Nell awoke with the determination to write the letter to Belle before noon. She had decided to approach the letter in an unemotional, "Just-the-Facts-Ma'm" manner. After several false starts, she composed something she thought would do:

Dear Belle Sheppard,

On March 23, 1939, in Memphis, Tennessee, Julia Edith Campbell was born to Charlotte Jane Campbell. Father unknown.

The baby girl was put up for adoption immediately by the mother who was using the stage name, Lola Bell. The baby was adopted by Leon and Edna Smith. Leon died of alcohol complications in 1954. Edna Smith lived until 1980.

In 1957, a detective hired by Bess Campbell of Kansas City, located Edie Smith, originally Julia Edith Campbell, in Southaven, Mississippi, living with her 2-year-old daughter. Two weeks after being contacted by Miss Campbell, Edie abandoned her daughter to the care of Bess Campbell.

I am that daughter.

Are you Julia Edith Campbell?

Sincerely,
Mary Nell Campbell Floyd
Floyd Farm

Blue Fork, Arkansas 72633
mnf@floydconstruction.com
479-555-1234

She read through the letter twice then set it aside. She'd look at it again tonight, show it to Walter, make any revisions, and put it in the mail tomorrow morning. She lay back on the couch and promptly fell asleep.

~~~

Walter returned home shortly after noon to find Mary Nell sleeping on the couch. He tiptoed through the house to the kitchen to fix himself some lunch. He smiled at Bitsy's paintings, thinking again how lucky they were to be close to their grandchild. His anger at his son bubbled up again. He really could understand divorce – people sometimes grew apart. But you don't divorce your children. As far as he knew, Dub had made no attempt to contact Bitsy since he left. Walter was ashamed of him. This thing Mary Nell was going through brought Dub's behavior into focus. Dub better be dead or held incommunicado. It was the only way Walter could forgive him.

He chopped up vegetables for his salad, hitting the cutting board harder as he felt his disappointment and disgust with his son's behavior rise. He hadn't finished with the celery when Mary Nell walked sleepily into the kitchen.

"Are you chopping it or beating it into submission?"

"Both I guess. Sorry to wake you. You okay?" He scraped his partially mashed vegetables into his salad bowl.

"Yeah. Didn't sleep much last night. I wrote a draft of the letter I'm going to send to Belle Sheppard, then fell asleep." She looked around, dazed. "What time is it anyway?"

"Almost twelve-thirty. Want some salad?"

"No. Thanks though." She poured a cup of coffee and sat down at the counter. "After you eat, would you read my draft? I'm trying to stay unemotional but factual."

"Sure will. Where is it?"

"Next to the laptop." She drank her coffee, watching Walter eat. "Is this the 22nd?"

"No, hon. Today's the 23rd."

"Goddamn. Not that slick little bastard today on top of everything else." Mary Nell slammed her hand on the counter

"What are you talking about?"

"That damned lawyer, Billy Yates, is coming here this afternoon. I have to sign some papers about probating the will. Think we should wait on that now that we've found Edie, er, Belle?"

"Dunno. Ask the slick little bastard."

"Funny. I guess I better meet with him. Damn, damn, damn."

"Want me to hang around?" He finished his salad and began cleaning up the counter and sink.

"As a matter of fact, I do. I don't think you believe me about what a horse's ass this guy is. He'll be here in half-an-hour. And I've gotta get dressed. Would you make a fresh pot of coffee? If I lace it with enough bourbon, he might just seem tolerable."

~~~

Billy Yeats arrived in the same shiny suit and skinny tie he'd had on the first time she saw him. And every time since. His smirking condescension was nauseating. She shot glances at Walter to see his reaction, but he'd played poker long enough to know how to control his face.

"Mr. Floyd. You certainly have a fine spread here. I admired your glossy cattle as I drove in, and I saw some fine examples of horse flesh in your pasture. You must be rightly proud of all your holdings." Billy Yeats cast his eyes at Mary Nell and back to Walter. "I imagine it takes a tight rein to keep everything under control."

Walter swallowed hard. "Oh, I've found most things flourish with the proper care and handling." He glanced at Mary Nell whose face had stiffened. "A firm hand calms the excitable and gives comfort to the steady." With that pronouncement, he folded his hands across his belly and leaned back into his chair.

Mary Nell watched him. Oh, he was good. She had to keep her lips pressed together to hold in a chuckle.

Billy was oblivious. "Now, Mary Nell, I know this is not how you want to spend your afternoon, dealing with your dead aunt's estate. But she did leave this to you, believing you would do right by it. So I need you to sign some papers." He looked at Walter and said, "The probate process is very stringent. I'm sure you understand."

"Oh, certainly. We must all follow the proper processes." Another self-satisfied look crossed Walter's face.

Mary Nell saw the twinkle in Walter's eye for a moment, but he pulled himself back in character quickly. She was actually enjoying this show. She'd yet to say anything beyond hello. How would she play it? She chewed her lip as Yeats continued explaining his own importance in the "probate process."

He was saying something to her. She stirred and listened. He got the papers out. She said in a small voice, "Could I have a minute to read them, please? Walter always tells me that I should read things before I sign them." She held back batting her eyes. She didn't want melodrama. A glance at Walter showed his eyes smiling approval. Two could play this game.

She took the papers and read through them, half-hearing Yeats' obsequious flattery of Walter and Walter's self-satisfied paternal pompousness. It lightened her spirits.

As she laid the papers down, Mary Nell gave Walter a "watch this" look, then turned to Yeats. "I do have a couple of questions, if that's all right." Yeats nodded. She straightened up, "It seems to me that I remember Walter saying the standard fee-base for the attorney was substantially less than 15% of the value of the estate." She turned sweetly to Walter, "Isn't that right, honey?"

She turned back to Yeats, "I also seem to remember that Missouri probate court meets in Missouri, not Hawaii." She picked up the papers again and flipped through them until she found her spot. "Royal Hawaiian Hotel for ten nights? Round trip air fare from Kansas City to Honolulu?" She leaned forward toward him, unable to contain herself. "Now, Mr. Yeats, I suggest you get your skinny little ass back to Kansas City and revise these papers before you ask me to sign them. Or I'll be writing some little letters to the Missouri Bar Association." This time, she did bat her eyes.

His jaw dropped. He looked to Walter for help, but Walter only gurgled in his attempt to stifle his laughter. Yeats stood up, grabbed the stack of papers, and stalked out of the house.

Walter erupted. "Haw-Haw-Ha! Batting your eyes, Mary Nell? That was too much."

She leaned back, crossed her hands on her stomach, and intoned, "A firm hand calms the excitable and gives comfort to the steady."

After they revived, drank some heavily laced coffee, and discussed what to do next with Mr. Billy J. Yeats, Walter said quietly, "Hon, I read your letter. I think it's fine. Send it. We can drop it at the post office on our way to dinner."

She cupped his cheek in her hand. "Yes."

# Part III: The Look-Back

*The look-back is the action of the dog going
away from the shepherd to gather in sheep that
are apart from the main flock*

# Chapter 21

*"That cowboy's been spendin' a lot of time at the café. Guess he's tired of his own cookin'."*

*"Betty's been buyin' some new clothes over at Dress It Up. Dotty said she's been in there two-three times."*

*"Well, it's about time. She's been draggin' around in sackcloth long enough."*

Buck stopped by the café many evenings for dinner. He and Betty had built an easy friendship since he told her his story. She liked using him as a sounding board for ideas about menus and promotion of the café. She knew his presence prompted talk from The Ladies – she'd overheard them once or twice. But she didn't care. It was nice to have a friend.

As he got more comfortable with her, he dropped some of his tough-guy act and increased his use of multi-syllabic words. After she ribbed him about it, he told her that she would be well advised to cease her defamation of his character, "None of my cohorts would be amenable to working with a pantywaist."

"Pantywaist!" She laughed again just thinking about it. She was waiting on the few stragglers to finish their lunch so she could leave the place with her newest part-timer and run up the street to the new shoe store that just opened.

Just as she was about to leave, Shawna and her mother came in. Betty knew Diane Taylor only slightly. Diane was several years older than Betty, and they had different sets of friends. She hadn't seen Diane in months, but she'd heard from Shawna that her mother worked for the new vet in town.

Betty took their order and stayed to chat for a minute. She teased Shawna about monopolizing her brother's time. Shawna said there was little to monopolize, between work and school.

Betty decided to try again to hit the shoe store, but as she opened the door to leave, Buck entered. He sat at the counter and ordered coffee.

"What are you doing, loafing this afternoon?" Betty asked as she set his coffee in front of him.

Buck shrugged. "Don't I get a coffee break?"

"I guess you do if you have so little to do. Or that much help."

"Hah. Don't I wish. No, I have to meet a farmer about some pigs." He eyed her skeptical raised eyebrows. "Really. Walter's talking to this farmer about supplying organic pork to the store, but he and Mary Nell had to go out of town. So he asked me to talk to the farmer." He looked at his watch. "And he's late."

Shawna and her mother came to the counter to pay their check. Shawna saw Buck and smiled. "Mom, have you ever met Buck Toomey? Buck, this is my mom, Diane Taylor. Buck runs the greenhouse for Mr. Floyd."

Buck looked past Shawna to her mother, extending his hand, then froze. "Were you Diane Watson?"

She frowned, "Do I know you?"

"Oh, yeah. You did. Buck, er, Ben Toomey. You used to call me Benny Two-time."

Diane's partially extended hand went to her mouth. "Oh my God! You're the Buck that Shawna's always talking about?"

"Yeah, I've been Buck a long time."

"I'll be damned. I never expected to see you again."

"No. Bet you didn't."

Diane picked up the change Betty handed her and started to the door but turned back to stare at Buck. "Damn. Benny Two-time." She sighed and turned again.

"Wait, Diane. How is she? Is she okay? Married? Kids? Happy?"

"I'm not sure you deserve an answer, but Sara's fine. Married to a great guy, two kids. Got a degree in bio-chemistry and works in the oil business in Houston."

"Thanks, Diane. One last question. You know how heavy I was drinkin' then. I keep thinkin' somebody was pregnant when I left. Was it Sara?" His eyes carried hurt, uncertainty, and guilt.

"No. It was me. With this one," she patted Shawna on the shoulder.

"Ahh, thank God," Buck sighed. After another breath he said, "I heard about John. I'm sorry. I liked him."

She considered him for several moments before she hooked her arm into Shawna's and left.

"She doesn't like you very much," Betty observed as she refilled his coffee.

He nodded several time, "She has good reason not to."

~~~

*"I heard Diane Taylor and Buck Toomey got into a fight in the café."*

*"Naw, it wasn't a fight. She just cut him cold."*

*"Why? What'd he do to her?"*

*"Not to her. Her sister. Married her. Then ran around on her and left her."*

*"Wonder how Shawna feels about Uncle Buck now?"*

Shawa's description of Buck's and Diane's confrontation left Rusty confused. "How did your mom know Buck?"

"He used to be married to my Aunt Sara."

"Why's your mom so mad at him?"

"He cheated on Aunt Sara. Drank too much. Then ran off with some 'floozy' my mom says."

"Doesn't seem like him. Long time ago."

"I know. That's what I told Mom. She mumbled something about skunks not changing their stripes."

"That's pretty cold. People do change."

"Yeah, I know. I think she was just shocked to see him again."

Rusty squeezed her hand. "Well don't let that get in your way with Buck. He was your uncle once, after all."

She took a mock swing at him, but he caught her fist and pulled her to him in a hug. "Let's go for a walk."

Shawna took off her apron, picked up her purse, waved goodbye to Tommy, and left the store.

Rusty yelled, "Bye, Dad. See you at home by eight."

Shawna took Rusty's hand and swung it a few times. "Maybe you should say something to Betty. She and Buck seem to be getting pretty close."

Rusty shook his head vigorously. "Nope. We've got a pact. We don't give each other advice about 'matters of the heart'." He placed his free hand over his heart.

"Don't be a jerk." She took a few steps before saying, "So Betty's never said anything about me?"

"Well, she told me I better be nice to you. And that you're too good for me."

"And don't you forget it."

~~~

Walter had convinced Mary Nell to drive up to Springfield with him. He thought it would do her good to get out of the house. She was truly trying to relax, but checking phone messages, email and the mail box was occupying far too much of her time.

"I'm glad you came with me today, hon."

She patted his arm, "Thanks for talking me into it. It's good to get away. I even left my Blackberry at home."

"I noticed. Hey, look over there." He pointed at a border collie circling behind a flock of sheep. "I didn't know anyone raised sheep out here."

Mary Nell turned around to watch the dog out the back window as they drove past. "Looks like an inexperienced dog. His outrun arc was too shallow. He cut off half-a-dozen sheep."

"I don't think I remembered to tell you that I saw Lulu trying to work chickens. They put up with her for a while, then one of the roosters flew at her. She was so surprised. She's not used to flying sheep."

"Buck said he's never trained her. It's all instinct."

"She must be from good working lines."

Mary Nell looked at him in surprise. "Crap. I forgot to tell you. Lulu's from BellWhether Kennels."

Walter shot a quick look at her before turning back to the road. "You're kidding? When did you find that out?"

"One day I was playing ball with Lulu, and Buck and I got to talking. He said she'd come from Plainview, Oklahoma. Then he said it'd be a good place to hide. Like the *Purloined Letter*."

"Guess it was."

"Yep. Guess it was." They rode in silence for a while before Mary Nell said, "I've been thinking about getting a dog."

"Lulu?"

"Yeah. And Bitsy. I'd like her to really know a dog."

"Fine with me. You know that. Hell, get two or three. We've got the room."

"One'll do to start." She patted his arm again.

When they got home, Mary Nell walked out to the road to get the mail. She sorted through it as she walked back to the house, then stopped and held up an envelope. The return address was BellWhether Kennels. She tore it open and pulled out a single sheet of stationary printed with the BellWhether Kennels name and logo. The page was divided in half by a blue line. Above the line in bold black ink was written the single word "YES". Below the line in blue ink and a different handwriting was written "Give her some time – Sally O'Neill."

Mary Nell stared at the page for several minutes before saying loudly, "Damn her! Damn her!" She carried the letter to Walter, shoved it at him and said, "Look! Damn her!"

He took the sheet and studied it, glanced at Mary Nell, and looked at it again. "Well, you got your answer."

Her eyes narrowed, and she snorted, "Yeah. I did. I got a damned answer all right." Her voice shook as she asked, "How much do I have to take?"

Walter pulled her into a hug, "I don't know, hon. I think you just take what you have to."

Mary Nell reached for her Blackberry. She called Gina. Tapping her pencil impatiently while she waited, she planned what she would say. She had rehearsed it so thoroughly, that she blurted it out as soon as Gina answered, talking over the top of Gina's greeting.

"Sorry. Hi, Gina. Let me catch you up." She described the letter she had sent and the one she received. "Find out everything you can about Sally O'Neill, will you? I want to know where she came from, what she does, what's her relationship to Belle, everything. Fast."

"Should have something by morning. I'll call you."

Mary Nell hung up without a farewell.

# Chapter 22

*"Hear Mary Nell's out gadding again."*

*"Somebody said she was going to Oklahoma."*

*"Why would anybody want to go to Oklahoma?"*

Driving west toward Oklahoma, Mary Nell passed through her favorite part of the state. The Boston Mountains. Old mountains. Rounded and womanly. Not all angles and sheer rock like those she grew up with. They were what convinced her to move to Arkansas. They felt safe. And she felt exposed as she drove out of them.

She was still trying to digest the information Gina and Tony had found about Sally O'Neill. That added to her discomfort. She had needed to find Belle, to settle Bess's estate if for no other reason. But she was only being nosy about Sally. It felt intrusive.

She convinced herself again that it was necessary to learn all she could, and to remember it. So she began to review the facts of Sally O'Neill that Gina had sent her:

> Sally was born in 1936 in Dodge City, Kansas. She lived there until 1984 when she bought BellWhether Kennels and moved to Plainview, Oklahoma.
>
> While she lived in Dodge City, she worked for 27 years for the sheriff's department, first as a clerk, then moving up to deputy sheriff. In 1984, at age 48, she was shot in

the knee by an escaping rapist, and pensioned off with permanent disability.

Sometime in the late 1950s, Sally had begun training border collies to herd cattle at her grandparents' ranch. She trained and trialed stock dogs for about ten years.

In the mid-1970s, she was sent for training to work with man-tracking bloodhounds, Later she trained and bred them herself. Her connection with the sheriff's department helped her be accepted by law enforcement agencies, and between the dogs and her pension, she was able build a good business.

Belle Sheppard moved to Plainview with Sally in 1984, taking over the border collie side of the business. There was no record of Belle Sheppard before 1984.

Mary Nell was determined to meet and talk with Sally O'Neill. The addendum to Belle's letter seemed to invite it.

Mary Nell pulled into the spot that the map labeled Plainview without seeing anything that resembled a town. She drove up and down the highway until she saw someone in a pickup truck and flagged him down.

"Is this Plainview?"

He shrugged, "What there is of it."

"It's not a town?"

"Nope. Just a delivery address. Lookin' for somethin'?"

"BellWhether Kennels."

"Ah. Yeah. Go down about a mile to the third road on the right. Turn there and go out another couple miles. Can't miss it."

"Thanks. Any place to eat around here? I'd like to get some lunch before I go to BellWhether."

"Yeah. Stay on this road about seven miles. You'll come to Edith. There's a diner there. And a motel."

"Edith is the name of the town?"

"Yeah. If you want somethin' besides diner food, you can go on into Buffalo."

"Diner's fine. Thanks. Um, third road and right. Two miles."

"Yeah. Good luck."

Mary Nell drove down to the third road and looked for something to differentiate it from every other road in the area. How would she find it on the way back? She thought a minute, then got a sheet of neon green poster board from the trunk. She'd have to tell Walter that it paid off to carry Bitsy's art supplies with her. She tore the board into strips, and wove them, green side out, through the strands of barb wire, pushing the barbs into the paper to hold it. It probably wouldn't hold through a wind storm, but today was calm. She thought it would stay long enough for her to have some lunch.

In Edith, she found the diner easily. It, the motel, and an abandoned gas station were the only buildings on the highway. She went inside the diner, past yellow plastic fly strips, and found a clean if old interior that was somehow welcoming with its gray and white marbleized Formica-topped tables and chrome-legged chairs.

"Get you somethin'?" A sixty-something round woman in a print cotton dress and a bib apron appeared before her with a glass of water. Her gray hair was pulled back into a bun, her face was pleasant, and her shoes were sturdy.

"A cup of coffee to start. And could I see a menu?"

"Today's menu is cheeseburger, club sandwich, or meatloaf plate."

"OK. Then what's on the meatloaf plate?"

"Mashed potatoes and gravy, green beans, and cornbread."

"That'll be fine. Thanks."

The woman went behind the counter and dished up Mary Nell's food. Within minutes, she delivered a heaping plate of comfort food. Mary Nell took a bite of the meatloaf and smiled, "Almost as good as mine."

"Almost. Hah!" The woman chuckled as she refilled Mary Nell's water glass. "How'd you ever come to be in Edith?"

"I'm going over to BellWhether Kennels. And I was hungry. A farmer I flagged down in the non-existent town of Plainview sent me here."

"Joke around here is that Plainview ain't."

Mary Nell stared at her for two long beats before she got it. "Ah. Right."

"Gettin' a dog at BellWhether?"

"Maybe. First I want to talk with Sally O'Neill. Know her?"

"I've been knowing Sally and Belle since they first moved out here. 'Bout 25 years ago."

"The kennel has a very good reputation."

"You won't find finer dogs. They're very careful. Only breed the best. Sell off the "less than spectacular", as Sally says, and keep the stars to breed."

"So what are they like—Sally and Belle?"

"Sally O'Neill never met a stranger. Talk your ear off. She's the one who trains bloodhounds, mostly. Works with the law enforcement teams they send here to learn how to handle man-trackers. She used to be a deputy sheriff."

"Hmm. She sounds interesting." Mary Nell didn't tell the woman that she knew anything about Sally. She hadn't told her anything new yet, but maybe she would.

"Oh, Sally's a pistol. For all she has to walk with a stick, she can out-go most folks. Still goes out in the brush to lay trail for the training sessions."

"How about Belle Sheppard?"

"Belle's quiet. Reserved. Doesn't talk much. Let's Sally talk for her. Concentrates on the border collies. Has won 'bout every trial in the country. Breeds beautiful dogs – workers with good temperaments. I've got one of her pups. He didn't want to work as hard as Belle wanted him to, so she neutered him and gave him to me for a pet. She won't breed them if they won't work. Says she won't dilute the breed. Shep's the best dog I ever had. Smart! I swear he reads my mind."

Mary Nell finished her lunch while the woman talked. She thanked her for the lunch and the information, and headed back to Plainview. She hoped her green fence was still there.

It was. She found it easily and turned down the road to the kennels. She began to practice what she'd say to Sally. But the first person she saw had to be Belle. She looked so much like

Lottie, Belle's mother and Mary Nell's grandmother, that it was uncanny. She was in a pasture with a young border collie and several sheep. She carried a long staff that she used to move the sheep. She was doing close work with the dog, training it not to bite or harass the sheep.

Mary Nell was mesmerized. She watched for several minutes before it occurred to her that if Belle was out here, then she wasn't with Sally. And Mary Nell wanted to speak to Sally alone.

She drove to the building marked Office, and went inside. A pair of inquisitive brown eyes turned toward her. They belonged to a woman in her seventies with short gray hair, glasses, and a big smile.

"Help you?" she said, looking up at Mary Nell from the desk where she was working.

"I'm Mary Nell Floyd. I'm looking for Sally O'Neill."

"My God! I guess you are." She struggled to her feet and stuck out her hand. "Sally O'Neill And you look so much like her it takes my breath."

"I saw her out in the pasture. She looks like my grandmother."

"Likely. But you look the way she did fifteen, twenty years ago."

"I'd like to talk to you. Can we meet somewhere? I know she's not ready for me and I'm not sure I'm ready for her, but I want to know about her. Will you?"

"Yes. That's probably best. I'll meet you tonight at 6:00 at the diner in Edith. Get a room in the motel there. It's plain but clean. We can eat at the diner then go to your room to talk in private. You know how to get there?"

"Yeah. I ate lunch there."

"Then you met Bea. Her real name is Josephine Murphy, but she seemed so much like Aunt Bea in the Andy Griffith Show that we started calling her that. Most people think it's her real name."

"I met her. She's a character. Good cook."

"Yep. She only fixes two or three things a day, so you have limited choices, but they're always good."

"Oh, I don't mind eating there again. I could do with a good cheeseburger."

"Good. I'll see you there at six. You better go now. She'll be in soon."

Mary Nell thanked her again and left quickly. She saw Belle walking out of the pasture as she drove away.

She went back to Edith, rented a room on the back side of the motel and lay down on the bed. "I saw her. I saw her. I saw her" kept rumbling through her head. She would be crazy before 6:00 if she didn't stop. She found her Blackberry and called Walter. "I saw her, Walter. I didn't talk to her, but I saw her." She told him about the town of Plainview, the diner, the motel, Bea, Sally and her dinner plans. "I'm going to lie here and try to be calm until I meet Sally for dinner. I'll call you afterwards."

"You've been busy. I'm proud of you. You're doing great."

"Thanks, hon. You okay?"

"I'm fine. I'm going to meet with Buck and Betty this afternoon. They've got an idea they want to discuss, they said. They seem to be getting along real well. I guess it's time for Betty to find somebody else. Our son's not likely to come back."

"I'm glad to hear you say that."

"Yeah. It's hard to admit that Dub's a disappointment. Oh well. I've got to run. Call me later." Walter again waited for Mary Nell to hang up first.

Walter headed to the café. He wished he could be there with her, but he knew this was something she needed to do herself. He couldn't imagine how it must feel to see your mother for the first time in over fifty years, not even knowing she was your mother until a few months ago.

He might not have had much money growing up, but he had plenty of love from both parents. His dad was a good father, attentive and caring and willing to be the parent, give guidance and discipline. Walter patterned much of his parenting after his father. His mother was indulgent with her boys and demanding of the girls. Typical.

After he got through his teens, he was happy to see traces of his parents in himself – in looks as well as behaviors. It must feel very lonely not to have that connection, that lineage. Or not to have a role model. He was lucky, he thought, in so many ways.

Betty and Buck were waiting for him. Buck rubbed his palms on his thighs as he said quietly, "Thanks for coming, Walter. Before we tell you our ideas, I need to give you some background information about me." Buck then told him quickly the story he'd told Betty, adding that he'd been married to Shawna's aunt and left her for another woman.

Walter listened closely. As Buck finished, he looked Buck in the eye and said, "I don't know that man. I know the one I've been working with for the last several months. And I like and trust this man."

Buck looked relieved. "Thank you. I told you that for two reasons. One, to apologize to you for not being honest about who I am. And two, to let you know that I know quite a lot about food and restaurants."

"OK. So what's your idea?"

Betty said they'd been talking about even with all the fresh and healthy foods that were available in town now, most of the locals still bought canned green beans and iceberg lettuce from the Food King. Buck added that he'd talk to the new vet when he took Lulu in for shots, and she told him her sister's kids were getting fat on the school lunches.

"So, we thought we need to do something to teach the locals about new foods and new ways to prepare old ones." Betty continued. "But we don't want them to feel that we're coercing them or ridiculing them."

Walter rubbed his neck, "The building next to the café is nearly ready for occupancy. Is there something we could use it for?"

Betty and Buck grinned at each other and Walter. "We hoped you'd think of that. We thought about some sort of cooking school. Only not that formal. Maybe demos that correspond to the specials in Grandpa's Greens."

Walter made a couple notes on the notepad he always carried in his shirt pocket. "Let me talk to some folks. I think I heard about somebody trying something like this. Keep thinking. I like it. I'll get back with you in a week or so."

He closed his notebook and put it back in his pocket. He stuck his hand out to Buck, "And Buck, I'm proud to know you. It took courage to tell me your story. Now it's time you quit holding your past against yourself."

After Walter left, Buck and Betty settled back to chat. Betty said, "You seem so much, I don't know, maybe lighter than you were when you first came to town. I used to think there was something slightly sinister about you."

"Humph. No, not sinister. Just sad and guilty. Always had a nagging fear Sara was pregnant when I took off and I'd left behind a child. But I was too afraid to find out the truth. Guess I thought that not knowing for certain freed me from responsibility.

Betty reached a hand across the table and touched his arm. "I can see that. You must have been afraid to know and afraid not to know."

"Most of the time I didn't think about it. But I always felt the guilt riding me. After talking to Diane the other day, I let the guilt slide off."

Betty squeezed his arm again. They sat in silence for a few moments before Betty said, "This is an odd request, but I wonder if you'd mind if I told your story to Mary Nell. I think she might need to hear it."

Buck looked puzzled, but nodded. "If you think it would help her some way, go ahead."

~~~

*"I hear Rusty and Shawna are both going to the University."*

*"Yeah, Rusty's goin' into Ag, specializin' in growin' stuff in water. Hydro somethin'."*

*"I'm not sure about that hydro stuff. God meant plants to grow in dirt."*

*"Shawna's goin' there too? You watch, they'll be married before long."*

*"Marriage ain't the worst that can happen."*

*"She gonna study food science, whatever that is. Whoever heard of such? You raise stock and you butcher it. You raise crops and you harvest 'em. What's science got to do with that?"*

# Chapter 23

By a few minutes before six o'clock, Mary Nell was seated at a table in the Edith Diner. She wished she'd thought to bring a bottle of wine from home. She hadn't realized that she couldn't buy any around here, and she could use a glass of wine. Maybe it would loosen Sally's tongue, too.

Oh, well, she'd drink iced tea and try to settle herself down. She was stirring sugar into her tea when Sally arrived. Sally and Bea hugged, and Sally handed Bea a paper bag before heading to the corner table to join Mary Nell. As Sally arranged herself in the chair, Bea arrived with a bottle of Merlot and two glasses.

Mary Nell grinned, "You read my mind. I was just wishing I'd brought some wine from home."

Sally poured them each a glass and raised hers in salute: "Here's to lubrication."

"Amen," chimed in Bea.

Mary Nell ordered a cheeseburger and Sally the meatloaf. After Bea left them, they looked each other over. Sally spoke first, "Just so you know, I told Belle that you'd come and that I was meeting with you. I decided it was wrong to hide it."

"Since you're here, I take it she didn't object?"

"Object? No, that's not Belle's way. But I think it's fine with her. I've been her spokesman for a long time. It's just natural that I do so now."

Mary Nell nodded as she bit into one of the best cheeseburgers she had ever eaten. She would have to bring Walter here. He thought cheeseburgers were the food of the gods.

"So what do you want to know" Sally took another swallow of wine and studied Mary Nell across the top of the wine glass.

"Everything. Start anywhere. Just tell me what you know. I'll ask questions if that's all right."

"Fine." Another sip of wine. "I'm really hungry though and I'd like to eat some of this great food before it gets cold while I embark on a soliloquy. While I eat, you tell me about you."

"Deal. Just let me have a few more bites of this cheeseburger. My husband would kill for this."

"So you're married?"

"Uh-huh. Walter Floyd. Been married thirty-three years. We have two boys, Walter Allen Floyd, Jr., Dub, and Jeffery Ian Floyd, Jif. Dub's divorced, living in Chicago. Has a five-year-old daughter, Bitsy, who's my joy. Jif's in the Air Force, stationed in Kuwait. Not married." She bit off another piece of cheeseburger and chased it with a couple of perfectly crisp French fries.

"And you live in Blue Ford, Arkansas? Odd name."

"Blue Fork. Not quite as bad as Ford." She smiled fondly, "I'd love to hear the tale Walter would dream up to tell Bitsy about why the town was named Blue Ford."

"You have a good marriage? Your expression when you speak of your husband says that you do."

"That's right. I do. I'm very lucky with my husband. And my granddaughter. Everyone else has their moments."

Sally laughed with delight. "You have your moments, too, I'm sure."

"Oh, I do. I'm short-tempered and impatient. I hate condescension and arrogance. I'm too blunt with people, and I hide my fears behind my bluster."

"You must have some good qualities, I expect." The merriment danced in her eyes.

"I'm honest and loyal and hard working. Cripes, I sound like a border collie."

"You know border collies?"

"I had one that I loved. Gem. I got sheep, did trials. When I lost her, I lost interest. No, that's not right. I missed her too much to go on without her."

"You should have gotten another pup."

"Probably, but I didn't. Then time got away from me, the sheep got old and died, and I ended up with no dog and no flock."

"That's fixable."

"I know. Maybe one of these days. I've been thinking about it."

"OK. I won't push." She took a final drink of wine. "I've finished eating. If you have, why don't we take our wine to your room and finish our talk?"

The motel room had few amenities, but it was clean and had two comfortable chairs and a table in addition to the bed.

Mary Nell brought glasses from the bathroom and poured them each some wine. She adjusted the thermostat, asked Sally if she needed anything, then dug out a notebook. "I hope you don't mind if I make notes. I will forget too much if I don't write it down."

Sally shook her head. "That's fine. I'm used to it. Belle takes notes when I say good morning."

Mary Nell looked surprised. Sally continued, "From the little I've seen of you, I think you've inherited more than your looks from your mother. But you can judge that for yourself."

Sally took a sip of wine and started to talk:

"I met your mother in 1960, in Dodge City, Kansas. She had run away from a relationship with a horrible man, Johnny Benton. He was alcoholic, physically abusive, and in and out of trouble with the law. She hitchhiked from Memphis to Dodge City, stopping many times to work a few days or weeks along the way. She came to Dodge City expecting to find the cast of "Gunsmoke" in residence, but she got a job at the sheriff's office anyway. I had just been promoted to deputy.

"She was afraid of Benton. She'd been hiding by using a number of assumed names. In fact, she hired on at the sheriff's office calling herself Edie Bell. When we got to be friends, she convinced me to help her change her name legally. She thought it would make her harder to find.

"I was used to calling the guys in the department by their last names, and I hate the name Edie. Sounds like a lounge singer. So I called her 'Bell.' Always have.

"Anyway, I was active in herding trials with border collies. My grandparents had a cattle ranch. Working dogs were members of the family. I took Belle with me to meet my grandparents and watch the dogs work, and she was hooked. I taught her what I knew about training dogs, then she surpassed me. She was a natural. She trained, trialed, and started saving money to buy the best dogs she could to start her own breeding program.

"Pups from top dogs sell. Her financial situation improved. She seemed happy and content.

"I got involved with bloodhounds about the same time Belle started doing so well with the border collies. I was sent to class in Georgia with a top bloodhound trainer to learn how to handle man-tracking bloodhounds. Sheriff said it was because I was good with dogs. I think it was mostly that nobody else wanted to go to the swamps of south Georgia in August.

"I went. I fell in love with the big sniffers. I went on to train my own dogs and then those for other law enforcement agencies.

"Belle and I built and shared new kennel facilities at the ranch. We got along fine.

"Then two things happened at almost the same time. Belle heard from old friends that Benton was out of jail again and looking for her. And I got shot."

Sally leaned back in her chair, stretched her shoulders, and suggested Mary Nell pour more wine. She pointed at a paper bag she had set on the bed. Mary Nell opened it and found two more bottles of Merlot.

"Planning on a late night?" she asked as she uncorked the bottle.

"Didn't want to run short," Sally replied with a shrug. When they'd both settled back into their places, Sally continued.

"I was shot in the knee by a mean son of a bitch who wanted me to suffer. I had several surgeries, but the best they could do left me with a limp and a cane. I'd never be able to go back to police work.

"They pensioned me off with a permanent disability. I'd worked there since I was twenty, so I get a good monthly stipend. Between the kennels and my pension, I was financially okay.

"Belle was terrified that Benton would find her. She decided she needed to change her name again and get out of Dodge." She stopped and looked at Mary Nell, "You getting all this down?"

"Yes, I'm okay. Thanks."

"Well, then. I asked around to see if I could locate an established kennel somewhere that we could go work at, or buy. Found the place in Plainview. The owner was getting too old to keep up with all the work. He had some great bloodhounds. I'd bought pups from him. A mutual friend hooked us up. I made him a good offer for the place, and he took it.

"Only thing holding us back was a new name for Belle. She tried on dozens, writing them, saying them. I finally told her that I didn't care what she named herself, I'd call her 'Bell' whether that was her name or not.

"She stopped in her tracks. She said that 'Belle' can be a first name. I agreed. Then she got that half-grin that I've seen playing on your face, too. She said I'd given her another idea. How about calling the kennels BellWhether? She likes word play. You know what a wether is?"

"Mmm. Neutered male sheep."

"Yes. So then she played with other names until she hit on Sheppard. Belle Sheppard of BellWhether Kennels. I liked it.

"So we moved here in 1984. Belle was forty-five and I was forty-eight. Nobody here knows her by anything but Belle. Our kennels are thriving, we breed and train good dogs. It was a good move."

Sally reached for her wine glass. "I imagine you have questions."

Mary Nell puffed out her cheeks and slowly blew out the air. "Where to start? Oh, what happened to Johnny Benton?"

"He died in jail about five years after we moved here. Never found her."

"Was he my father?"

Sally studied Mary Nell's face, "Yes."

"Did she send me to Aunt Bess to protect me?" Mary Nell's voice cracked mid-sentence.

"Yes. He had beaten her for years, but he'd never touched you. Then he started threatening to kill you. Said she paid more attention to you than him. The letter from your Aunt Bess arrived in the middle of that. Belle had been planning to take you to the nuns in Nashville."

Mary Nell nodded. She understood what you'd do to protect your child. She looked at Sally's kind face and said, "But why…." Her voice broke and she swallowed a few times.

"Why didn't she come get you? Why didn't she contact you?" Sally's voice was soft.

Mary Nell nodded.

"I don't think she knows. She told me that she never intended to leave you there. I think fear and time got in the way. By the time she'd conquered her fear, time had moved on too fast and too far. Twenty years ago, you were what? Thirty-five?"

"Yes."

"Would it have changed anything at that point if your long-lost mother appeared in your life then? That's about as soon as she could have done it. Benton was dead. She didn't have to protect you any more. But she thought it was too late."

"I don't know." Mary Nell shrugged. "I just don't know."

Sally gathered her things. "I think you've had enough for tonight. Belle would like to meet you. Come out to our place about nine tomorrow morning. If you want to. If you can't, she'll understand." She stood up and flexed her knee. "I hope you'll come."

She gave Mary Nell a long hug, then walked to the door. "Try to get some sleep."

Sally got into her car and finally allowed her eyes to brim over. She mumbled a prayer, "Oh, God. We humans can twist ourselves into such places. Help them set it straight."

Mary Nell continued to sit at the table, reading through her notes. At least her mother wasn't the unfeeling monster she'd feared. She felt raw. And as kind as Sally had been, her words opened up layers of scar tissue that had never properly healed.

She managed to find her Blackberry and call Walter. She told him what she'd learned from Sally and that she was invited to meet Belle in the morning.

"Oh, hon. I know this is hard on you. Just remember, most of life isn't about villains and victims. Just people caught in unfortunate circumstances doing the best they can. I know you'll do the right thing."

"Thanks. I wish I had your faith in me."

"Luckily, I have enough for us both. Get some sleep. Call me tomorrow."

She quickly disconnected.

# Chapter 24

Mary Nell was awake before five o'clock but forced herself to stay in bed until five-thirty. The diner opened at six, and she planned to be first in line for coffee. A quick shower later, she was at the door of the diner by a few minutes before six.

Bea was inside making several pots of coffee. She saw Mary Nell, let her in the door, and said "Coffee in a few." Mary Nell slumped into a chair. Bea examined her closely, "You stay up all night talking to Sally?"

"No, she left before nine. But I finished off the wine. And had a restless night." She looked up as Bea poured her some coffee. "Better make it a double."

"From the looks of you, I'd say a triple."

Mary Nell liked the easy friendliness of Bea. They chatted about unimportant matters while Mary Nell ate eggs, bacon, biscuits and hashbrowns in addition to several more cups of coffee. She never ate breakfast. Today she couldn't get enough. Her body must be stoking up for the coming encounter.

When she left the diner, it was only seven o'clock. What could she do for an hour and a half before time to go to the kennels? Then a ray of sunlight caught her in the eye, and she thought of Bitsy. She'd call her before she went to school.

Cheered by the thought, she opened the door to her room and finally found her Blackberry under the covers of the bed. She sighed, and placed the call. Betty answered and chatted for a few minutes, asking her how it was going and giving encouragement. Then she put Bitsy on the phone.

"Oh, Grandmary! Where are you? I miss you!"

"I'm in Oklahoma, Bits. I'll be home either tonight or tomorrow."

"Do they have good dolls in Okelhoma?"

Mary Nell smiled, "I don't know, Bits. I'll have to look. What would you classify as good?"

"Huh?"

"What kind of doll do you want?"

"I dunno, Grandmary. One from there that you can't get here."

Mary Nell's grin grew wider. "OK, Bits. I'll see what I can do. What are you going to do today?"

"Well. I'm going to school. Then the café. Then home. Will you come see me when you get home?"

"Yes. I'll see you after school tomorrow."

"Oh, good Grandmary. I love it when you get me from school."

"You do? Why?"

"Because nobody else has a Grandmary to get them. They just have mommies and daddies."

A stab of sadness hit Mary Nell. Damn that Dub. She took a deep breath, then forced a smile into her voice, "I'll see you tomorrow, punkin'. Have fun today."

"OK, Grandmary. You have fun, too. Lookin' at dolls." And with a giggle, she handed the phone back to Betty, who waited until she heard a click before hanging up.

Driving back to Plainview, Mary Nell thought again about parents and children. Because she'd never known her biological father, and her adoptive father was an alcoholic asshole, popular psych said she'd pick a bad husband. But she hadn't. She'd married the kind of man who turned into the kind of father she'd wanted. Not that he fathered her. He didn't. He treated her with respect, as an equal. But he parented the boys, the Taylor boy, Rusty, and Bitsy.

Maybe we make too much of traditional family roles, she thought. Maybe "responsible, caring adult male" can be played by many different men in a child's life. Maybe Bitsy would be okay. She had Walter, Rusty, Tommy, and now Buck.

That reminded her of the story Betty had told her about Buck and the guilt he had carried thinking he'd abandoned his child. Maybe Dub felt some guilt. Maybe Belle did.

She drove onto BellWhether Kennels property and her body turned to stone. She couldn't do it. She didn't know what to say. The woman obviously didn't want anything to do with her or she'd have looked for her years ago. Her thoughts tumbled over each other until she noticed the dashboard clock. Nine o'clock. She pulled into a parking place, got out and nearly fell. Her legs wouldn't cooperate. Fear gripped her around the waist. She nearly doubled over. She thought she would vomit.

After several deep breaths, she was able to stand and take a few steps. "Come on, now. You can do it. Just try," she whispered to herself as she opened the door to the office. It was empty. Then she heard a cane tapping in the hallway.

"Sorry I'm late. I had a phone call from a prospective buyer. Come on back." Sally gestured back down the hall.

Mary Nell hesitated. Sally said, "It'll be all right. Come on now." A few steps later, she turned to see if Mary Nell was following. "She's as afraid as you are. Come on. I'll be there."

Mary Nell thought she knew exactly how Daniel felt on the way to the lions' den. She followed Sally into a large comfortable room. Windows on the north wall admitted light, soft rugs on the hardwood floors absorbed noise. The result was a bright softness, like a sunny day after a snow. Sitting at one end of a beige leather couch was the woman she'd seen in the pasture who looked so like her grandmother. Her mother. Belle.

Mary Nell entered the room, hand extended. Belle stood and said, "I'm Belle Sheppard. Welcome."

Mary Nell's response was automatic after years of business meetings and cocktail parties. She shook hands with her mother, "Mary Nell Floyd. Pleased to meet you." When she realized the inappropriateness of that old standby greeting, she felt her knees start to buckle again. If she couldn't even say "hello" properly, she might as well leave.

Sally put a hand on Mary Nell's elbow and steered her to a chair. She looked from Mary Nell to Belle and saw the same expression: terror. "Look, you two. You're going to have to get over your fear if you're going to make any headway. I'm going to make some tea. I've had too much coffee. Try to talk to each other while I'm gone."

Mary Nell found some courage, "I didn't even know you existed until Aunt Bess died last fall. I found you as quickly as I could."

Belle said stiffly, "I've always known you existed. But I didn't know how to find you."

Mary Nell's neck stiffened, "Aunt Bess was alive until September. She always knew where I was. And she still lived in the same house until she died."

"Oh, your physical location wasn't the problem -- I didn't know how to find you emotionally. I still don't."

"I'm not sure I know what you mean."

"I imagine that you're feeling many things about me. Anger at my giving you up, hurt that I did, guilty thinking it was your fault, cheated because you didn't have a mother. Close?"

"Yes. I've felt all those things."

"And all those feelings are genuine and understandable and real. And all of them condemn me."

"Mmm. Yes, I see that."

"So how do I build a relationship with someone whose very being exposes my guilt?" Her voice broke, and she looked at her hands in her lap.

Mary Nell rubbed her forehead and sat silent. After a couple of long minutes, she said, "The same way I build a relationship with someone whose very being exposes my abandonment." She took another deep breath. "Even though I didn't know about you, I was abandoned by the father I never knew and the "mother" who died. Janet, your sister, claimed me. I thought she was my mother. She died when I was eight, leaving me with grandma."

Belle looked stricken, and Mary Nell's eyes glittered with unshed tears. "You didn't know about Janet?"

Belle shook her head slightly. "No."

Mary Nell said quietly, "All I can think of is something my husband said last night. He said most of life isn't about villains or victims; just people trying to do the best they can."

"I don't know what to do."

"I don't either. But I think I have to try. We've made a start. Let's see where it goes."

"As you wish."

Mary Nell's eyes snapped, "No, Belle. Don't make this all about me."

"You're right. I've anticipated your scorn for so long that I am seeing it where none is intended."

"I understand that. I've been terrified of your rejection. I thought you wouldn't want to know me."

"But I do."

"And I don't hate you."

"You were right, Mary Nell. We've made a start. Let's take it slow. I for one need time to adjust."

"Me, too. I think I should go now."

Belle stood. "Let me walk you to your car."

She led the way down the hallway to the kennel office. When they entered, they were greeted with whining and yipping. "Damn kid. I told him not to leave the pups in here when nobody was around. They could get hurt." Belle's irritation flared then dimmed. She reached to pet one of the five bouncing border collie puppies jumping at the sides of the pen.

"Oh, they're beautiful. May I hold them?"

Belle nodded, and Mary Nell held one after the other to her face, rubbing her cheeks in fur, scratching behind ears and tickling tummies. As she set the last one back in the pen, she said "Thanks. It's been too long since I've been around puppies."

Belle smiled. "These are out of one of my champion bitches. Their sire is my favorite multi-titled stud. Probably the best litter I've ever whelped. I usually keep a litter in the office for a while to socialize them. These guys are almost big enough to go to new homes. I'll keep the best bitch, I expect. I think this blue merle one with the heart-shaped mark on her head has the most nearly perfect conformation I've ever seen. She's got great bone, beautiful angulation, and already moves like a star."

Mary Nell was surprised at the length of Belle's response. It was the most words she'd said yet.

After a final pat on each black and white head, Mary Nell impulsively hugged Belle. "Thank you. And please thank Sally for me."

Belle patted her back, squeezed her hard, then held her by the upper arms and looked into her face. She nodded, "Thank you."

Mary Nell drove away, feeling drained, but peaceful. She had pushed past the expected. She stopped along the side of the road to call Walter and tell him she was on her way home. She asked him to hang up first.

# Part IV:  That'll Do

*The term "that'll do" is used to release the dog from whatever it was doing and to get it ready for the next activity*

# Chapter 25

Three weeks later, Buck had gone to Fayetteville to look at commercial kitchen fixtures suitable for a cooking school when his cell phone rang. It was Walter asking if he'd mind stopping by Delta Air Cargo and picking up a shipment. Walter said it was addressed to Mary Nell, but she was off for the day with Bitsy. He didn't know what it was.

Buck agreed. When he finished his business, he drove to the airport and located the air cargo area. The woman at the counter said she was happy to see that someone had come so quickly to claim the shipment. Buck nodded, signed the papers and drove around to the loading deck.

With the crate in the back seat of the truck, he drove back to Blue Fork, smiling in anticipation of Mary Nell's reaction.

Walter was outside when Buck drove up. He looked at the crate, and grinned. "She's gonna be surprised."

Buck hauled the crate out of the truck and sat it in the shade. Walter went for Mary Nell. She came out the door, wiping her hands on a towel she held.

"What's so important I had to come right now?" She looked up and saw Buck. "Hey, Buck. What's up?"

He handed her the envelope that had been taped to the top of the crate.

She looked puzzled, but opened the envelope. As she pulled out the papers, a whining noise came from the crate. Looking from Walter to Buck and back, she started reading the top paper as she walked to the crate. It was a Transfer of Registration from the American Border Collie Association. She stopped reading and bent down to look in the crate. Two dark brown eyes looked back.

She fumbled with the papers as she tried to open the crate. Buck leaned over, opened the door and lifted a squirming black and white ball of fur into her arms. She sat down hard. She looked at the puppy's beautiful blue merle markings then back at Buck and Walter again. "When did you do this?"

Walter shook his head. "I didn't."

Buck grinned, "Me neither. Read the papers. Maybe they say." He took the puppy and rubbed her belly.

Mary Nell read the registration form. It was a transfer of ownership from BellWhether Kennels to Mary Nell Floyd of the border collie bitch, BellWhether's Unforgotten Treasure. The second page was in invitation to a Herding Instinct Test next month at BellWhether Kennels. A final page was a yellowed piece of stationery with a gaudy letterhead.

Mary Nell looked at it briefly without reading it, then shaking her head and resolving to look at it later, she stuck all the pages back in the envelope and stuffed it into her jeans pocket.

Turning toward Buck, she opened her arms wide. He deposited the puppy into her lap. As she was about to speak, Bitsy dashed out of the house.

"Grandmary! I lost you." She stopped short and dropped next to Mary Nell. "Oooh! It's a puppy!" She looked at the puppy's face carefully. "Look, Grandmary, she's got a heart on her head." She pointed out the black shape between the ears, in the middle of the white blaze that ran from the tip of the nose, between the eyes and ears and disappeared into the white collar at the neck. "Her name is Heart," she decreed.

Mary Nell patted both Bitsy and the puppy on the heads, then stood and walked back to the porch. She watched Bitsy, Walter, and Buck tickle and play with the pup.

"Heart," she said quietly, smiling at the puppy's antics and feeling her own heart pound and push a lump into her throat. She turned toward the door, trying to decide if she wanted coffee or a stiff drink, when she shoved her hands into her pockets.

She felt the stiff envelope she'd put there earlier and pulled it out to examine again its contents. First, the transfer of ownership. Then the invitation to a herding instinct test. And finally that yellowed piece of stationery she'd glanced at earlier.

She looked carefully at it and saw the logo of The Long Branch Motel in Dodge City, Kansas. Underneath the logo she noted the hand-written date, April 4, 1960. Then she tilted the page to the light and began to read the faded ink.

"Where the hell is Matt Dillon when you need him?"

# About the Author

Kathy Wagenknecht lives behind the nursery she operates just outside Little Rock, Arkansas, with her three border collies, two Cardigan corgis, and a talented painter.

Visit her website at **kathywagenknecht.com**, or learn more about her nursery at **www.whitewagonfarm.com**

10914441R00117

Made in the USA
Charleston, SC
15 January 2012